S0-BDO-643

MYSTERY   10-81

Heald
 Murder at
Moose Jaw

DISCARDED

Newark Public Library
Newark, New York 14513

Murder at Moose Jaw

By Tim Heald

Fiction

MURDER AT MOOSE JAW
CAROLINE R
JUST DESSERTS
LET SLEEPING DOGS DIE
DEADLINE
BLUE BLOOD WILL OUT
UNBECOMING HABITS

Non-Fiction

HRH: THE MAN WHO WILL BE KING
THE MAKING OF SPACE 1999

Murder at Moose Jaw

TIM HEALD

PUBLISHED FOR THE CRIME CLUB BY
DOUBLEDAY & COMPANY, INC.
GARDEN CITY, NEW YORK
1981

All of the characters in this book
are fictitious, and any resemblance
to actual persons, living or dead,
is purely coincidental.

ISBN: 0-385-17754-2
Library of Congress Catalog Card Number 81-43126
Copyright © 1981 by Tim Heald
All Rights Reserved
Printed in the United States of America
First Edition in the United States of America

For John Macfarlane and the lost weekend

Newark Public Library
Newark, New York 14513

Murder at Moose Jaw

PROLOGUE

The personal railroad car of Sir Roderick Farquhar was a glorious anachronism in a country otherwise short on such eccentricity. It had been rescued from the breaker's yard by Sir Roderick himself and restored to its former luxury under his own scrupulous supervision. That night as it rattled out of Moose Jaw station en route for Swift Current, Medicine Hat and the Pacific coast it was the only antique in the train, a single memory of the old Canadian Pacific lingering on among the shiny new blue-and-gold coaches of Via, the Canadian answer to Amtrak and British Rail. Along its varnished purple side the gilded legend "Spirit of Saskatoon" glittered in the moonlight. Inside in the refurbished galley, jars of plovers' eggs and pots of Oxford marmalade jostled the Gentleman's Relish and bottles of lychees in kirsch. The wine cellar was stocked with port from the House of Warre and claret from Château Lafite, and in the dining saloon, in a drawer of the Georgian sideboard, there were two boxes of Cuban cigars, nine inches long, a present from the president.

Outside in the vast emptiness of the northern night, the silence was broken only by the steady thump and clatter of the train and the lonely cry of a loon. Inside the ticker tape chattered spasmodically but did nothing to disturb its owner, who had dined well. Being head of the Mammon Corporation had its compensations. Sir Roderick had been operated on for ulcers and had long ago discarded the last of his four wives, but he was rich and he was powerful. Mammoncorp was the largest conglomerate in the Dominion, the fifth richest in North America and the tenth in the world. The Farquhar family fortunes, while below the billion mark, were, nonetheless, adequate and his annual income was at a level appropriate to his needs.

Tonight he had dined with his private secretary, Prideaux, who had then retired to his modest quarters in another part of the coach. Sir Roderick had made two telephone calls, one to Caracas and the other to Zürich, before putting down his Havana, replenishing his cognac and retiring for the night. As always he drew his own bath. This had become a ritual and no one else in the world, not wives, not mistresses, not manservants, had ever adequately managed it. He liked the water to be warm but not hot and he liked it to be of such a height that when his frame was immersed the surface came to a level no more than a centimetre below the auxiliary drain hole. The bath was an eighteenth-century Florentine tub rescued from a decaying palazzo five years before, not only commodious but a sound investment too. It was his habit to pour the water, place the latest copy of the *Wall Street Journal*, the Toronto *Financial Post*, the London *Financial Times* and the city pages of *Die Welt* and *Asahi Shimbun* on the walnut reading tray, add not more than three drops of his Balenciaga bath oil and stir it judiciously with the three remaining fingers of his left hand. Only then did he divest himself of his monogrammed silk robe and enter the waters gingerly but with the keen anticipation of the genuine sybarite. He took his pleasures with the true seriousness of the convert, for he was a son of the manse and had been brought up strictly on porridge and corporal punishment.

This night between Moose Jaw and Medicine Hat his pervading sense of loneliness and failure was numbed as usual by the external warmth of the bath water and the internal warmth of the alcohol. The steam rising from the surface of the ocean between chin and toes was so fragrant that he breathed it in deeply, savouring the scent of pine needle and jasmine and feeling so contentedly sleepy in so peaceful a manner that no one would have believed that he was inhaling the odour of death.

Next morning at six, Amos Littlejohn, the burly Louisiana-born ex-heavyweight boxer who had been senior steward to the president of Mammoncorp for the past ten years, knocked on the door of his master's bedroom. The silver tray which he carried so cleverly immobile in his left hand supported a goblet of fresh grapefruit juice and a pot of newly brewed coffee made with a half-and-half mixture of Jamaican and Brazilian beans. There being no answer Littlejohn gently opened the door and raised the blind. When he had done so he turned to the bed and was sufficiently surprised by its pristine emptiness to spill two or three drops of grapefruit juice. The aroma of lavender bags reproached him and he hurried away in search of Prideaux.

The personal secretary was not amused at being woken so early but on hearing the reason he hurried from his closet and followed the steward to Sir Roderick's boudoir. Once there he turned pale and dabbed limply at his brow.

"The bathroom," he said. "We must try the bathroom."

The bathroom door was not locked since Sir Roderick's position guaranteed a privacy born of extreme fear. The two men entered apprehensively, to find Sir Roderick Farquhar reclining placidly in his ancient bathtub. The grubby water lapped the peak of his paunch in time to the motion of the wagon's progress. The newspapers lay across the bath as neat and unsullied as the bedroom sheets. The face of Mammoncorp's president wore a benign expression of happy repose that neither observer had ever previously witnessed.

He was, of course, extremely dead.

CHAPTER 1

Simon Bognor gazed wanly at the lake. It looked cold. Across its
bleak grey surface a tall unwieldy ferryboat was churning towards
the ring of islands which shielded the harbour from the worst of
the storm. On a clear summer's day, Bognor knew, you could see
the spray from Niagara Falls, simply by peering hard from the
twenty-fifth floor of any hotel in town. In winter you were lucky
to see beyond the end of your nose. He rubbed his stomach reflectively and put a piece of croissant in his mouth. The room was
warm. Hot indeed. Despite the Arctic outside it was possible for a
man to stand stripped to the waist wearing only a pair of striped
cotton pyjama trousers knotted nonchalantly below the navel
with a bow. Bognor knew a shop near Jermyn Street in London
where they had not yet discovered the elastic waistband. He
sighed. He had no overcoat. It never snowed in November. He
had rung the High Commission in London before leaving, spoken
to the Minister for Public Affairs no less.

"Never snows in Toronto before December," he had said. "Besides, Canada's centrally heated. And you don't have to walk anywhere."

Bognor in early middle age was not a pretty sight. His hair was
going fast and his waist, never a dominant feature, had finally
disappeared. His complexion was unclear and he had more than
one chin. He buttered another piece of croissant. The trouble
with this sort of place, he thought to himself, was that they never
gave you enough bloody butter. It came in a plastic capsule designed to appeal only to those whose life was dominated by their
cholesterol count. He thought of ringing room service for more
but decided against. He would have a yoghurt shake for lunch.
There was a place in the depths of the Sheraton Centre where

they did an apple-blossom yoghurt shake unlike anything he had
ever tasted.

He had been here before. Not many months earlier there had
been an untidy business involving a colleague in the Toronto con-
sulate whose body had been discovered deep-frozen by a cross-
country skier in a conservation area a few miles to the north of
the city. For reasons too eccentric to be accurately described as
reasons, Bognor had suspected Sir Roderick Farquhar of smuggling a new and powerful form of LSD across the Atlantic in jars
of Gentleman's Relish. In this he had been mistaken. It had been
the work of Farquhar's personal assistant and neither the Canadian nor the British Government had been amused by Bognor's
aspersions. Farquhar was too significant to be messed around by a
middle rank investigator from the British Board of Trade. The
RCMP, however, had belatedly come round to his point of view.
Bognor's intervention had thrown up a lot of dust and some of it
had been gathering on the Mounties' files. Farquhar, it transpired, had a past. The files pointed to prewar Latvia and a sinister accommodation with pro-Nazi elements. Later there had been
an undoubted involvement in the Viennese black market, prosti-
tution in Batista's Cuba and regular Paraguayan business trips
which had continued until the year of his death. Before he arrived in Halifax, Nova Scotia, one autumn morning in 1951
Farquhar had had at least five names. Not one of them was
Farquhar.

Bognor yawned. As a result of all this he was held in a certain
awe by the men of the Mounties, besides which he was the Board
of Trade's expert on Canadian affairs. He had only been in Canada for six weeks on the Gentleman's Relish case but that was at
least five weeks longer than anyone else in the board's offices in
Whitehall and it gave him a reputation. He did not discourage
this. He was not good at his job and he was therefore forced to
grab at anything which could convince his colleagues to the contrary. Accordingly he made a point of studying the hockey results
in the small print of his *Daily Telegraph*. He would then irritate
everyone by remarking from time to time: "Leafs shut out the
Sabres yesterday" or "Lafleur scored three Wednesday" or "Seems
Orr's knee broke down again." All of which meant nothing at all

at the Board of Trade, and precious little to Bognor. It did, on the other hand, impress them, however marginally. Like most Englishmen they knew very little about Canada and were not eager to know more.

Bognor finished the croissants and put on yesterday's shirt and a clean tie. He resented laundry bills, regarding them as needlessly expensive. At home his washing was done by his new bride, Monica. New bride, old girlfriend. She had been part of his furniture for as long as he could remember. They had finally married for reasons of which neither was entirely sure. It was something to do with feeling too old to live in sin. Also they both, though neither had admitted it, felt a vague desire to be unfaithful and this was easier, and safer, within wedlock than without. Negative reasons, Bognor conceded, but then he had seldom done anything for positive ones. They had married at Chelsea Registry Office on a sodden morning six weeks ago. Parkinson, his boss, had been best man, held the ring, brought along a brace of red carnations and taken them to lunch at Santa Croce in Cheyne Walk by the Thames. They had become euphoric on champagne and lasagne verde.

"*O tempora! O mores!*" he muttered, fumbling with a knot of his tie. Any semblance of control over his life seemed to have gone long ago. Ever since that terrible moment at Oxford when he had fatuously been deflected from his decent, ordinary, humble ambition to become a bureaucrat. He would have been an admirable civil servant. He was designed for indecision, for referring matters to colleagues and committees, initialling reports without comment. He could in time have become a master of the art of office filibuster, of saying nothing, importantly. He might have achieved a minor medal. Or more. Become Sir Simon. Something vital but unspecified in the Ministry of Posts and Telecommunications, or Employment. Instead he had listened to the man at the Appointments Bureau and ended up in a branch of what was laughingly called Intelligence, a department cloaked in the half-baked pseudo secrecy of a basement office in the Board of Trade. All cloak and no dagger. Codes, ciphers and, over the years, a half dozen or so bizarre assignments that had started tamely and ended . . . distressingly.

He put on his jacket and glanced at the front page of the *Globe and Mail*. The main story appeared to be about a committee appointed by the Ontario government to investigate traffic pollution. They had immediately gone to investigate traffic pollution in the Bahamas. The *Globe* smelt corruption. Alongside the piece there was an account of a boat trip up the Yangtse by the Peking correspondent. Bognor had noticed on his previous visit that the *Globe* had little time for abroad in general but made up for it by keeping a man in China. He supposed that this was because China was the only place on earth where there was never any news—or if there was, no one was allowed to report it.

The phone rang—a soft, catlike sound.

"Bognor," he said, briskly.

"Hi, Si. Good to have you back. It's Pete Smith. RCMP. We met on the last Mammon case. Do you have a moment?"

"Yes. Of course." Bognor swore to himself. Of course he had a bloody moment. More like several moments. All the time in the world.

"Shall I come round?"

"Up to you. I could meet you somewhere. I ought to buy some boots, and a hat. I was caught unawares."

"Canada's kinda cold in winter, Simon."

"I heard. Your men in London didn't seem to think it was winter yet. If I go and buy something woolly I can meet you afterwards."

"Okay, Simon. You can buy your gear at Simpson's, then we can meet on the roof."

"The roof?"

"Sure. There's a coffee shop up there. Haven't been for years, but I guess they'll fix coffee."

"Right," said Bognor. "Shall we say an hour, then? I'll go up to the coffee shop and ask for you. And if you don't recognize me I'll be the one in the new boots."

He could charge the boots to expenses. There would be a row with Parkinson but he would get away with it in the end. Now that Parkinson had moved up a rung or two he was magnanimous. He had a bigger office and more pay and sometimes the ex-

asperation with which he regarded his subordinate was tinged
with affection. Or so it seemed.

Outside in the street the force of the wind took him by
surprise. It was snowing in what was locally known as "a flurry"
and it ripped into his face on gusts of urban gale frozen by its
long passage east across the prairies. Or south across the frozen
north. He wasn't sure. Geography had never been one of his
strong points. Wherever it came from, this was not the sort of
snow he was used to. *His* snow was a thin British drizzle that
turned to slush the second it hit ground or, just occasionally, left
a film of white dust redolent of Dickensian Christmas cards.
This snow was not at all the same. It stung. It came at you from
all sides and even when it should have been lying serenely in
your path it leaped up and hit you amidships. Looking about him
he realized that everyone else was dressed for it. Their lower legs
were encased in galoshes and "fun-fur" boots that looked as if
they had been cut from the living Yorkshire terrier. Their hands
were mittened and their heads protected by long scarves and fur
hats, tea cosey-shaped woollen things and balaclavas, their bodies
by melodramatic parkas and eiderdown-filled greatcoats guaranteed to keep you warm in a temperature of hundreds of degrees
below zero. By the time he reached the main railway station he
was beginning to lose feeling in the tip of his nose and fingers.
Somewhere he had read that a man's lungs could freeze in this
sort of weather and then explode like burst water pipes when they
thawed out. It was with enormous relief that he stumbled into
the womblike welcome of a high brass and glass structure belong-
ing to one of the many banks that lined Bay Street.

"By God!" he gasped, breathing heavily and rubbing his hands
between his knees to get the circulation going, "Bloody Arctic!" It
had now become incredibly hot. With a fine disregard for the energy crisis the bank appeared to be blowing hot air around its
building, as if it were trying to cultivate cacti. It was a tactic cal-
culated to bring on pneumonia in any normal man and Bognor
knew it. He feared he was suffering from terminal hypochondria
and that this was likely to precipitate a fatal attack. He was so
preoccupied with the tingling in his fingers that he didn't notice

the girl at first. His eyes were watering, blurring the passersby as they hurried down the escalators into the bowels of the building.

"Mr. Bognor." The girl seemed solicitous. She was very small, not more than about five foot two, swathed in a light brown fur which Bognor judged to be synthetic. Her boots were shiny brown and she had on a dark-blue beret, pulled down over the ears. Though none of her hair was showing she looked dark, almost olive-skinned. Her eyes were a light translucent blue and she wore very little makeup.

"Mr. Bognor," she repeated. "Are you all right?" She spoke with the distinctive accent of the Quebecois, a sound which was to French as American is to English. He felt flattered by this unexpected attention. He had always found Canadians unforthcoming, as anxious about social intercourse as the English were supposed to be. Torontonians most of all. Even they admitted to being in the crude vernacular of the place "tight-arsed."

"How did you know who I was?" asked Bognor, who rather prided himself on his chameleonlike anonymity, his effortless ability to blend into the surroundings. He had thought he was looking rather Canadian today.

"It's not important," she said. "Let's just say I was given a description, also a photograph."

"But you're not a Mountie?"

"No, of course not. Quite different. But we too have ways of finding things out. The description was very accurate. But it's not important, we're wasting time."

"Oh," said Bognor.

"You must buy a coat," said the girl, "or you will freeze. You English are crazy."

"Not at all," said Bognor, "*Pas du tout*. I was on my way to buy a coat. I left mine behind. Silly of me. I simply hadn't realized—"

She cut him short impatiently. "We must talk," she said. "It's very important."

"We *are* talking," he said, pinching his nose, to clear the brain. "But how did you know who I was?"

"That doesn't matter."

"Oh, but it does." Bognor's lucidity was returning, "You knew my name. We haven't met." He peered hard into the face, pert and gamine, tried to fathom the piercing eyes. "Have we?"

"We have friends in the RCMP. Your photo is in our files after the affair of the Gentleman's Relish," she said, glancing about her. "We must hurry. They may be watching. I must go now. We will see you tonight. Take this, and *au revoir.*"

Before he could complain further, the girl had turned and hurried away into the crowd. Before doing so, however, she had thrust a small white envelope into his hand. Opening it he saw that it was a theatre ticket: third row of the stalls for tonight's performance at the Royal Alexandra Theatre. He pocketed it, bemused, and set off down the escalator and then through the catacombs, the long lanes of boutiques and delis and underground trees and fountains which threaded the city's foundations like a rabbit warren. Ten minutes later he came out on the corner of Bay and Queen, made a quick dash across the street and emerged red and breathless in Simpson's shoe department. Just over half an hour later he looked almost Canadian. On his feet he wore a pair of waterproof galoshes over the brown brogues he had brought from London. He had a pair of padded mitts, a knee-length quilted parka and a green woollen hat with a bobble decorated by a ring of prancing caribou. He toyed with the idea of ski goggles and a pair of herringbone knickers, specifically designed for striding across the frozen wastes, but he decided they were too melodramatic. Far too melodramatic for coffee with Smith of the Mounties.

He was quite breathless when he reached the coffee shop. His parcels were encumbering, and he had taken a couple of wrong turnings. At the entrance a man in a Tip Top Tailors suit stood waiting.

"Si," he said, hand outstretched. "Great to see you."

Bognor grappled with his parcels and failed to extricate a hand.

"Nice to see you, too," he replied. He was almost certain he had never seen the policeman before in his life. He was lean and bony with an oversized nose and a weathered complexion. His hair was very short and he had a neatly trimmed ginger moustache.

"You take coffee?" he asked.

"Yes please." Bognor made to join the line-up which moved slowly past the unappetising displays of processed food, but Smith waved him towards a table by the window.

"You just set your bags down and rest your feet. How d'you like it?"

"Black, no sugar," said Bognor. He never had milk before lunch.

"Be right with you," said Smith.

The snow had settled patchily on the green copper of the Old City Hall roof just opposite. Bognor watched in idle fascination as the wind gusted along the guttering and teased the gargoyles. It was beginning to drift.

He thought of Sir Roderick Farquhar dead in his railway carriage between Moose Jaw and Medicine Hat, a fat corpse slopping around in the bath, depressingly unlamented. Death had been by bath oil. Bognor was no chemist, but someone who was had managed to insinuate a lethal substance into Sir Roderick's bottle of Balenciaga. Phosphorus trioxide, the lab report had said. Otherwise known as P_4O_6. At first they had thought it might have been supersaturated sulphuric acid, but that would have left burns. Farquhar had died from inhaling phosphine, produced by phosphorus trioxide crystals, more of which had been found in the bottle. The clever thing about the crystals was that they didn't turn into gas until they were mixed with warm water—28.3 degrees centigrade to be precise. The glass of the bottle was opaque so the old boy wouldn't have noticed anything, especially as he was invariably half cut after dinner. He wouldn't have known a thing till the phosphine hit him. By which time it would have been too late. He'd have been out before he could say Dow-Jones. Nice way to go for a nasty piece of work. Amos Littlejohn, the steward, claimed that the dead man had always poured the oil in himself. He also swore that that night's bottle was brand-new and sealed. The level of liquid confirmed this. The seal, like that on so many of Sir Roderick's personal effects, was wax, and seemed newly broken.

"One black coffee no sugar." Smith put the coffee down on the formica top of the table and smiled automatically. Bognor was glad they were on the same side. He had a cold-fish look that suggested a sinister expertise in the interrogation room.

"You making much progress?" asked Bognor, carefully pouring spilled coffee from the saucer back into the cup.

Smith peeled the top off a sachet of sugar and poured it fastidiously, then stirred with his spoon.

"I wouldn't say 'much,'" he replied. He took a sip of coffee and dabbed at the corners of the moustache.

"You get what you wanted?" He indicated Bognor's parcels, and Bognor nodded. Smith was clearly going to come to the point in his own time, ponderously and unhurried. That was fine by Bognor. He much preferred to let others make the running, so for five minutes or so the conversation followed a trivial course quite unconnected with the matter at the forefront of both their minds. Eventually Smith said,

"You heard what's happening at Mammoncorp?"

Bognor nodded. No holds had been barred in the internecine struggles in the Mammon boardroom and the warring factions were still at each other's throats. Quite apart from the antipathies of various directors, previously held in check by Sir Roderick there had been the unseemly squabbling of various relations of the dead man. None of his four wives was still living; the major beneficiary of his will appeared to be one of his later mistresses, a peroxide blonde presently residing in a white clapboard mansion overlooking Skaneateles Lake in upper New York state. This lady, unexpectedly cognomened "La Bandanna Rose," was actually a former fan dancer named Dolores V. Crump, and as soon as she had heard of Sir Roderick's demise she flew into town to defend her interests, with a sharp Manhattan lawyer riding shotgun. Bognor's latest intelligence was that though there was no way her purely financial situation could be threatened, power was going the way of Sir Roderick's son-in-law Ainsley Cernik, a handsome but supposedly stupid cipher dominated by the formidable women around him. But the situation was not fully resolved and there were a number of shadowy influences. The Canadian Government was said to favour Cernik, but the Americans were not averse to La Bandanna Rose, whose candidate, Colonel Crombie, had a place in Florida and was an admirer and acquaintance of

Ronald Reagan and Bob Hope. Bognor had himself been instructed to do all he could to further the ambitions of a third force, dominated by a handful of old-moneyed patricians from the wealthy Toronto and Montreal districts of Rosedale and Westmount. The leader of this group was an elderly Anglophile named Harrison Bentley. Privately Bognor regarded him as a "no-hoper" but he would, as always, do as he was told.

"Unholy mess there, Simon. Just awful." Smith shook his head sorrowfully.

"You think someone at Mammoncorp knocked him off?"

It seemed the logical question but Smith looked pained.

"You think that?" he asked.

"I don't know. It just seemed a good place to start."

"Who would have done it?" asked Smith. "No one benefits. Farquhar was a 'divide-and-rule man,' as you people say. Lookit, it's more than a month since he went and still they can't decide who takes over. No sense any of those guys killing him."

"Who then?" asked Bognor. He was deciding he didn't care for this man. He seemed far too sure of himself. Bognor disliked certainty. As far as he was concerned life was a tentative affair made up almost exclusively of doubts.

The Mountie leaned forward, his stomach bulging dangerously against the waistband of his trousers. "We know who did it, Simon," he said portentously.

"You know?" Bognor was incredulous.

"For sure." Smith maintained his expression of high seriousness, "This wasn't some boardroom piccadilly," he said, "this was your politically motivated crime." He leaned even further forward so that he was able to whisper. "Assassination," he said. "Those French bastards." And he returned himself slowly to a more normal posture, grinning.

"You *sure?*" Bognor frowned. "I mean, do you have proof?"

"We have all the proof we need, Si," said Smith. Bognor wondered what this meant. It could mean that the assassin had been caught, as it were, *in flagrante,* or it could mean that the Mounties had no proof whatever, regarding such a thing as a dispensable luxury. He did not voice these questions, however, contenting himself simply with a thoughtful nod. Then he said,

"But if you're so certain about this why don't you arrest them?"

The policeman grinned as if humouring a backward two-year-old.

"Like I said, Simon," he paused for a sip of coffee, "it's a political crime so those guys in Ottawa call the shots. They say 'no move,' because if we arrest the frogs who wiped Farquhar out, then Quebec will secede like there was no tomorrow."

"Ah."

"If it wasn't for the politicians"—Smith offered the word contemptuously—"they'd be inside by now and put away for a long time. They want to ruin this country. If they don't like it they should get out and go back to *la belle France* where they came from in the first place."

Bognor did not reply. In view of the prejudice it seemed most likely that there was no evidence against the Quebecois. He would have to proceed carefully.

"In the meantime," he said at length, "none of you will have any objection if I do some nosing around?"

"You just do whatever you want, Simon," said Smith. "Be our guest." He finished his coffee, and put on an expression of friendly menace. "Just keep your nose clean," he added, "and steer clear of trouble. This time we have it solved, and this time we're right. Happy to have your endorsement but as a matter of fact the work's all done. Job's finished."

"Right ho," said Bognor. "In that case I'll just take a look round, for form's sake, and concentrate on winter sports."

Smith smiled. Bognor smiled. It was obvious to each that their relationship was not rooted in trust, but for the time being they were both going to pretend. Bognor was good at pretence. Deceit was his stock-in-trade.

CHAPTER 2

Bognor's status was, at best equivocal. He had not been invited by the Canadians. He had invited himself. The arrangement had been finessed by various malleable officials at the Board of Trade in London, the Foreign Office, the Canadian High Commission and External Affairs in Ottawa. Papers had been shuffled, cocktails consumed, likewise lunch, until at the end of the day his involvement had been agreed and the question of who had instigated it was lost in bureaucratic confusion. His ostensible role was to help in solving the murder, no matter how much the Mounties might protest that it was already solved. His real and more secret role was to safeguard British interests within the Mammon Corporation. Mammoncorp had, over the years, made substantial investments in Britain, but in common with most British investments these were yielding lower and lower returns. Men like Farquhar were fed up with the mother country. It was all very well for his fellow billionaire Ken Thomson. Ken owned *The Times*. There was prestige in that, but Mammoncorp was into beer, biscuits, textiles and, God help them, motorcars. Farquhar and his fellow directors would never have drunk, eaten, worn, let alone driven in, any of their British creations. They were second-rate and unprofitable and the plants were teeming with idle Marxists. Mammon had threatened to withdraw on many occasions but Farquhar had possessed a residue of sentiment for Britain. Now that he was gone, however, the pressure to cut and run would become irresistible and the only people who could be relied on to put old loyalty before new acquisitiveness were Harrison Bentley and his friends.

Bentley therefore was the first of the Mammon board to be subjected to the rigours of a Bognor inquisition. This took place

over tea, a meal which evidently lingered on in those reaches of
Toronto society which still took pride in behaving in a manner
more English than the English.

"Good day to you," said Bentley, opening the door of his enormous nineteen-thirties colonial Georgian mansion overlooking a
rocky ravine in the most expensive neighbourhood in town. Bognor was surprised to find that he was wearing a monocle. Also
that he spoke with only the faintest hint of a North American accent intruding on an exaggerated, plummy, clubman's English
which Bognor had not heard in years. Bognor shook snow from
his feet and crossed the threshold. He found himself irrationally
irritated by the monocle.

"Hello," he said, extricating a hand from a mitt and offering it
to his host. "Bognor. Board of Trade."

"You had a good journey I trust," enquired Bentley courteously. He was a man of about sixty, Bognor supposed. Silvery
grey hair, somewhat arranged, a long deep-lined face, tall with a
slight stoop, he had a look of James Stewart in one of the later
films. He also gave the impression that he knew it, and worked at
it. He might have been English but for the monocle and the
tweed suit. The check was too loud and the squares too wide.

"Yes, thank you," said Bognor.

Bentley helped him off with his coat.

"And how was dear old London town?"

Bognor frowned, not sure what answer was expected. "Pretty
much as usual I should say, actually," he tried, half-heartedly.

"Ah," said Bentley. He hung up the parka with a fastidious disapproval, then rubbed his hands together for a moment and said
"Ah" again. Then he repeated, "Dear old London town."

Bognor did not reply.

"Come on through, Mr. Bognor," said Bentley, stepping across
the highly polished oak floor dotted with elderly Persian rugs. A
crumpled Airedale rose sleepily from a corner and joined them.
"Muriel's just made tea," said Bentley. "We have crumpets.
Crumpets are quite extraordinarily difficult to obtain in this country, Mr. Bognor. Indeed, had I had the opportunity I would have
asked you to bring a consignment from Jackson's of Piccadilly."

"Jackson's closed," said Bognor. "*Ça n'existe plus.*" He didn't know why he said it in French. He guessed he did it to annoy.

"Jumping Jehoshaphat!" Harrison Bentley passed a hand across his forehead as they entered the drawing room, several hundred square feet of it complete with grand piano, real logs in the grate and a wife, faded, thin, long-suffering, seated demurely on a chintz chaise longue. "Muriel," said Bentley, "this is Mr. Bognor from London, England. He tells me Jackson's of Piccadilly is closed."

Mrs. Bentley smiled wanly and shook hands. "Gracious," she ventured, "that's too bad."

"I would have asked Mr. Bognor here to bring crumpets from Jackson's," said her husband, "but now it seems there's no point. Muriel found these in the mix shop opposite the Summerhill Liquor Store. Are they Canadian, Muriel, or imported?"

Mrs. Bentley said that she was afraid they were Canadian crumpets. Not at all, she implied, the same as English crumpets. She poured the tea from a handsome silver pot. The tea, she explained, was from Twinings. Bognor, politely, mentioned that Murchie's of Vancouver enjoyed a fine reputation for tea. Mrs. Bentley smiled, suggesting that while this might be so, it was not proper to mention the place in the same breath.

"Mr. Bognor is from the Board of Trade, come to tell us all who murdered Farquhar," said Bentley, spreading butter on his Canadian crumpet.

Mrs. Bentley favoured him with another of her insipid smiles.

"That was a dreadful thing," she said.

Her husband did not seem to agree. He did not say anything, but concentrated ferociously on the crumpet and did not look up.

"Do you have any theories?" asked Bognor, trying to push the Airedale away from his fly without its owners noticing. The dog refused to budge.

"Theories?" asked Bentley. "What sort of theories?"

"About who killed Sir Roderick. Who the murderers were? Are?"

"*Cherchez la femme,*" said Bentley unexpectedly. He had finished his crumpet swiftly and now dabbed at the butter around his lips, using the red-and-white spotted handkerchief from his breast pocket.

"I beg your pardon?" Bognor was nonplussed.

"I'm sorry." Harrison Bentley smiled courteously and made a little play of removing his monocle and polishing it. "I understood from your earlier remark that you spoke French. *Cherchez la femme*. Find the woman. There's a woman at the bottom of this, you mark my words."

"What makes you think that?"

Mr. Bentley coughed with exaggerated discretion. "Muriel," he said, "perhaps you'd be good enough to leave Mr. Bognor and myself for a moment or two. I don't think this is something you should hear."

Mrs. Bentley rose and did as she was told. She was not the sort of woman who answered back.

When she had gone Bentley said, "I don't know how Farquhar managed at his age. He was insatiable."

"I'm sorry?" Bognor helped himself, unbidden, to a second crumpet. They were not half bad.

"Women"—his host said the word with distaste—"all the time. Sometimes two at once. Maybe more for all I know. He was over seventy." He shook his head in a mixture of shock and admiration.

"What sort of women?" asked Bognor.

"All sorts. That nigger manservant used to pimp for him. He laid on the whores and Farquhar looked after the classier ones himself. I don't know what women saw in him, but, boy, they certainly saw something."

"But what makes you think his womanizing had something to do with his death?"

"Stands to reason. He just cuckolded one man too many."

"Who in particular?"

"Oh, I'm not saying anyone in particular," Bentley grinned, conveying to Bognor the impression that if he wished he most certainly could say someone in particular. "To be frank," he continued, "whoever did it performed a public service. We're well rid of him. I know one shouldn't speak ill of the dead but in his case I'm prepared to make an exception. It was particularly distressing to me that he should have been the holder of an order of knight-hood. His conduct was always a long way short of that becoming a gentleman."

"You didn't care for him?" Bognor found it easy to fall into understatement. He glanced out of the French windows and saw that it was snowing hard. The conifers at the end of Bentley's substantial garden were barely visible through the scudding flakes and under their thick coating of white.

"You could say that."

"But you were happy to work with him? You've been on the board of Mammon for aeons. How did you square that with your dislike?"

"I've never seen any reason to mix business with pleasure," said Bentley. "Farquhar was a considerable businessman. His ethics may have been questionable but he made money. That's what business is about, so I was content to go along with him on that score."

"Until more recently?"

"I'm sorry?" Bentley leaned forward as if he had not heard properly, "How do you mean 'more recently'?"

"I understood." Bognor paused to remove a crumpet crumb from between two front teeth, "I understood that Farquhar was threatening to take Mammon out of the U.K." Bentley thought for a moment. "Yes," he said thoughtfully. "Yes, that's about the size of it."

"Not something you were keen on?"

"Naturally not."

"And yet"—Bognor looked thoughtful—"you don't mix business and pleasure."

Again Bentley seemed not to follow the drift of what Bognor was saying. Bognor explained. "Taking Mammon out of Britain," he said, "made commercial sense. Your objections were entirely sentimental. Wouldn't you say?"

Bentley removed his monocle and blew on it. "There are times, Mr. Bognor, when a man's principles must override other considerations."

In the grate a log spat, sending an incandescent crumb on to the hearthrug. Bentley hurried to pick it up between forefinger

Newark Public Library
Newark, New York 14513

and thumb, threw it back in the fire, wincing slightly as he did. Bognor watched and considered the implications of this admission. He thought of Dr. Johnson and patriotism.

"Another crumpet, Mr. Bognor?" asked Bentley when he had eliminated the risk of fire. Bognor said he wouldn't mind if he did.

It was an unsatisfactory encounter. Part of Bentley's perceived code of gentlemanly behaviour was absolute discretion. It was not so much that he could not tell a lie but that he did not wish to be caught out in one. He preferred to imply everything while saying nothing. He was a master of the gracefully delivered slur, the smiling innuendo. "All cut and no thrust," Bognor remarked to himself as he trudged gloomily southward through the blizzard, his eiderdown overcoat insulating him from the weather as effectively as the walls of Bentley's Rosedale mansion. He had had nothing but waffle, protestations of loyalty to fellow directors, to the firm, to the old country, to everything in fact but the memory of the dead man. Bognor would be returning to Harrison Bentley at a later date. Of that he was certain. Not just because he had conceived a profound distrust for the man but also because of one intriguing discovery made just before his departure.

At about the point that their interview had ground jerkily to its conclusion Bognor conceived an urgent desire to pee. He wondered if it was possible to get back to his hotel room without relieving himself first and judged that it would be more prudent to use Harrison Bentley's loo instead. Besides it was Bognor's experience that you could learn a lot about people's character from their loos and bathrooms. Those intimate little rooms with their old school photographs, their framed cartoons, their soaps and unguents and mirrors and potted plants and select reading matter had often yielded clues to Bognor that he had not found in more public rooms where display was contrived, whose very function was to impress. Bentley told him that the downstairs cloakroom had fallen prey to some mechanical dysfunction caused by cold, so Bognor had been sent upstairs to the master bathroom, a luxurious affair with sporting prints and copies of *Country Life*. There was also a bottle of Balenciaga bath oil marked "*Mis en bouteille pour Sir R. Farquhar*—bottled exclusively for Sir R. Farquhar."

It was half full. Bognor frowned hard when he saw it. The report said quite clearly that the bath oil was—as the labelling suggested —bottled exclusively for Farquhar and certainly not for any Tom, Dick or Harrison Bentley. The report also indicated beyond all possible doubt that the bottle of bath oil found in the Spirit of Saskatoon's bathroom was the instrument of death.

It was this discovery and this alone which raised Bognor's spirits as he shuffled through the snow. In itself, of course, it proved nothing. He had not questioned Bentley about it because he already felt defeated by his evasions and simpering. He felt sure that Bentley would have produced an answer and that he would not have believed it. Consequently he preferred to leave the question unanswered and therefore alive.

"Balenciaga bath oil," he murmured. "Exclusive to Farquhar, and yet sitting for all to see in Harrison Bentley's bathroom." It made very little sense. The one thing a pseudo-English gent with a monocle would not do was bathe in Balenciaga. Maybe Muriel Bentley used it. He sighed and slipped on a patch of ice. That was not the point. The point was that the murder weapon or one just like it was brazenly on display in Harrison Bentley's bath-room. Circumstantial perhaps but just as incriminating as coming across a revolver or a piece of bloodstained lead piping. He sighed and brushed ice from his eyebrows. He felt like a baked Alaska in reverse—a warm, crumpetty interior and a frozen façade. The thought of baked Alaska cheered him up so that by the time he finally found a subway station he was actually humming a Verdi chorus and feeling on the borders of optimism.

"So clean," he murmured, admiring the pristine state of the station, "so punctual. But where's the charm in that?"

CHAPTER 3

Bognor arrived early at the Royal Alex but very nearly went away again. The current attraction was *The Mousetrap* by Agatha Christie. Bognor had seen it twice in London, on both occasions with aged aunts now deceased. This production appeared to be on a tour of North America and the cast included a number of not quite famous names of the British stage of yesteryear, most of whom he had supposed to be as dead as his aunts. The prospect was unappealing. He could remember nothing whatever about the play except that it had established records for longevity. It ran and ran and ran until it became a theatrical freak, like a TV personality "famous for being famous." It was certainly not a good play. Bognor remembered a detective in a fawn mackintosh. Had there been a butler? Surely not.

He remained, uncertain, outside the foyer for several minutes but eventually entered. It was too cold to stand around. He had no alternative source of entertainment, and his ticket was free. Free gifts were irresistible as far as Bognor was concerned. Besides, something might turn up. The girl had been pretty and, in so far as pretty girls could be, somewhat sinister. Perhaps he would see her again, though why she should choose such a bizarre rendezvous he could not imagine. Nothing venture, nothing gain, he thought reluctantly.

It was warmer in the theatre but only marginally so. It was a Victorian building and draughty. Gingerly he took off his eider coat and slipped it under the seat, then sat apprehensively not knowing what to expect except two or more hours of bored actors in a boring play. He sighed. He wished he were at home in the London flat with Monica. They could be drinking whisky toddies, anticipating a pile of lasagne. He did not want to be here. It was

absurd. He sneezed. Next thing he would be catching cold. Or
flu.

Gradually the auditorium filled. The rest of the audience appeared to view the prospect of two hours of Christie with more
enthusiasm than he did. Conversation buzzed. The air was thick
with Chanel. Women were in furs and jewels, their men soaked
in aftershave and, mostly, corsetted into tight waistcoats. Many of
those present looked the sort of folk one would expect to find
drinking sherry at Harrison Bentley's place before Sunday lunch,
after matins at the Anglican cathedral. This was Old Toronto at
leisure—Orange Anglo-Saxon Protestants. Bognor's row was full
by five minutes to curtain-up, except for the seat on his right.
This vacancy excited Bognor. The empty seat suggested what he
had hoped. In a moment a person would come and sit in it. A
person on her—or, less acceptably, his—own. That person would,
unless he were very much mistaken, be there for the express purpose of meeting him. Or so he hoped. If they were there for the
express purpose of sitting through *The Mousetrap*, he would be a
deeply unhappy man. He settled back into the red velvet and
tried to visualize the petite Quebecoise who had accosted him
that morning.

The play, scheduled to begin at eight, was late starting. But at
three minutes past when the house lights dimmed and the curtain rose no one had come to occupy the seat on Bognor's right.
This upset him. Onstage a drawing room, furnished and decorated in a style of which Harrison Bentley would unquestionably
have approved was greeted with a round of genteel but enthusiastic applause. The entrance of the first actors provoked more
clapping and even some isolated shouts. Bognor winced and
closed his eyes. It was going to be one of those nights. He was
sleepy. He had not come three and a half thousand miles to
watch a substandard rendering of a bloody awful Agatha Christie
whodunnit. He sighed and stretched and switched his mind over
to neutral. At least he could have a kip.

It could not have been more than ten minutes. Onstage they
were still in the drawing room, the women in twin sets and
pearls, the men in grey flannel bags. But it was not any *coup de
théâtre* by Miss Christie which jerked him back to con-

sciousness, it was a late arrival. All around him people were muttering irritably as the newcomer passed along the row towards Bognor, forcing members of the audience to lurch, cumbersome and complaining, to their feet. He was not managing with dexterity. "I'm sorry," Bognor heard. "Most awfully sorry. I'm sorry." These apologies were issued in a loud stage whisper which provoked a chorus of "Shushes" from the auditorium. At length the man, for it was, to Bognor's disappointment a male, stumbled over Bognor himself and fell, breathing heavily, into the vacant seat on his right. "Sorry," he said to Bognor, in the same stage whisper. "Traffic is just terrible. I was twenty minutes getting from Bloor to Adelaide." Bognor said nothing. He was aware of heavy-duty aftershave and a trace of a Quebec or Acadian accent. The man pushed his folded coat under the seat. Onstage a character called Giles said, "My God, I'm half frozen. Car was skidding about like anything." It appeared that Christieland was having cold weather too. Giles was afraid they might be snowed up tomorrow. Millie, mutton dressed as lamb in a skirt high above ugly thickset knees, clutched at the radiator and said they'd have to keep the central heating well stoked. This was greeted with a spatter of nervous laughter. On his right his new neighbour turned to him and said in the same accented whisper, "I'm sorry, but could I borrow your programme? I didn't get one." Bognor handed it over and wondered if he should try to stay awake. He decided he should remain awake and alert, not in order to appreciate the nuances of the play but just in case the whole elaborate charade of the theatre ticket should turn out to have some point to it. He assumed it had something to do with the man who sat in the formerly empty chair but he might have been wrong. There was an elderly couple on his left, she blue-rinsed, he bald as an egg. He saw no hope there. It was unlikely to be anything to do with the row in front. But what of the row behind? Bognor froze. He hadn't considered the row behind. Now he did so. He did not like the idea that an enemy might be sitting immediately behind him, even though the idea seemed somewhat farfetched. He liked it even less when, onstage, one the characters exclaimed, "A murder? Oh, I *like* murder." This struck Bognor as being at one and the same time silly and ominous.

"Thank you." The newcomer, whom he had quite forgotten in the excitement of his feverish apprehensions, was returning his programme. Bognor nodded warily and turned his attentions to the stage where events were assuming an ever more sinister turn. The inhabitants of a guesthouse were in the process of being marooned by snow, cut off from civilization and milkman. He knew how they felt.

As the curtain went down on the first scene, Bognor's neighbour got up again and left, whispering a further string of apologies but no explanation. Bognor wondered whether to follow him but decided against it. With his luck he would find himself following the stranger into the gentlemen's lavatory, an exercise which could only end in embarrassment. Misunderstanding. Complaint. Criminal charges. Deportation. It was not to be thought of. The man would, doubtless, return and Bognor eased back as the curtain went up on the same Olde Englishe room from whose windows cottonwool snow could be seen steeply banked. Two of the familiar-faced actors began to discuss the corned beef hash they had eaten for lunch. Bognor sighed audibly and shut his eyes.

He was a habitual dreamer, and he dreamed now, in colour, about a blizzard through which he stumbled for days on end, accompanied only by a team of husky dogs. It was a very dull dream and he was as bored by it as was possible for one to be whilst dreaming. Therefore he was almost relieved to be jerked awake by the sound of screaming. He was on the point of leaping to his feet when he realized that the screaming was entirely synthetic and coming from the stage, where the curtain was descending on the banshee figure of one of the actresses who had just stumbled on a freshly killed corpse. Bognor sighed and glanced to his right. The seat was still empty. As the house lights came on he looked down at the programme which lay on his lap folded back at the cast list. There was some handwriting on it, neat ballpoint blue, a simple message. "Mr. Bognor, meet me in the parking lot. Green Pinto. Will flash lights twice."

Aha. Bognor experienced a sudden quickening of the pulse. He was to be spared the longueurs of act two of *The Mousetrap*.

CHAPTER 4

The parking lot was immediately opposite the theatre, a flat expanse of concrete prairie stretching out towards the railway line and the lake beyond. Precious little hope of finding a green Pinto flashing its lights, thought Bognor, surveying the massed ranks of chrome and aluminium. He glanced back at the theatre and had a pang of regret. The play might have been bad but it *was* British. Now, standing out in this alien frost, he felt definitely homesick. He wanted Monica and a hot toddy and the *Evening Standard*. At this moment he would like nothing better than to be sitting on the floor of the flat wrestling with the *Evening Standard* word game. Or even Monica. He sighed just as a pair of headlights flickered at him. They came from a car idling over at the exit a few yards away. Impossible to see whether it was a Pinto, let alone green. The snow and the darkness were blinding. The lights flashed again and Bognor breathed in, did a metaphorical girding of the loins and sped across the road towards his rendezvous.

As he arrived, panting, the door was flung open. He hesitated, then got in rather heavily as a familiar stage whisper urged him to hurry. His bottom had hardly touched the leatherette before the car lurched out into a main road, turned left and spun away, slithering and complaining in much the same way that Bognor himself had crossed the road a few moments earlier. As they drew up at a red light, the driver glanced in the driving mirror and seemed to relax marginally. He turned to Bognor and, for the first time, spoke in his normal voice.

"I apologize," he said, "for dragging you away from the play. I could easily find you a ticket for another night if you wish." His accents were unmistakeably French Canadian. Bognor had not thought he liked the Quebecois accent but for the second time on his visit to Canada he was forced to concede that it could sound quite attractive.

"Please don't," he said, "I really can't be bothered with it. I can't stand all that fiddly plotting. And the acting is excruciating."

"It was the policeman." The French Canadian raced the protesting car away from the lights, crashing the gears as he did. "Sergeant Trotter."

"Ah yes, I remember now. Only he wasn't really a policeman." Bognor had a dim recollection of a dramatic denouement witnessed over a box of Black Magic chocolates twenty years before. Had he been with a girlfriend? Monica even? No, he could not have met Monica then. Or could he? He frowned. "I'm afraid I slept through most of the first act."

"I noticed." The driver smiled and Bognor had the impression of deep lines, a strong, attractive face somewhere in its forties, perhaps slightly younger, very dark. "Sergeant Trotter," he continued, "was some sort of lunatic. The real detective was Major Metcalf. Peculiar. I understood that the British police force sent superintendents to investigate murders."

"Do they?" said Bognor absentmindedly. "I suppose they do. Perhaps they didn't have superintendents in Agatha Christie's day. I'm afraid I'm not very observant about rank. I prefer the North American approach, Christian names all round and none of this pretentious nonsense about sergeants and majors and superintendents. By the way, I'm terribly sorry, I don't think I quite caught your name, I'm Bognor."

This remark was ignored. "I understand," he said, still driving too fast, still glancing twitchily in the mirror, "you work from intuition rather than deduction, Mr. Bognor. I can understand that you would not find Miss Christie's plots particularly appealing."

"They're all right in their way," said Bognor. "Only my experience is that real life isn't quite so neat and tidy. In fact, real life is an absolute shambles if you want my opinion. This particular case I'm working on at the moment being no exception."

They swung north on a multilane expressway. Bognor noticed a sign to the airport. He began to feel uneasy.

"I'm glad you think that," said his new acquaintance. "The Mounties seem to think they have it solved already."

"Sorry," said Bognor, "are we talking about the same thing? Do you know what I'm investigating? It's supposed to be something in the order of a secret."

"Ha!" It was not really a laugh, more of a snort. "It would be difficult to keep it a secret from me," he said, "and not very desirable. You see, the Mounties are sure that it was I who did it. That is what I wanted to talk to you about. I felt sure that you would have a more open mind."

"Not just open but positively blank," said Bognor. "You still haven't told me who you are or what it is that the Mounties think you did."

"Did anyone follow you when you left the theatre?"

"I don't think so."

"I don't think so either."

They had reached a spaghetti junction with a whole series of roads rising and falling, diverging and merging to an accompaniment of white arrows on emerald green signs. Cars moved from lane to lane inexorably, apparently sightlessly and very fast. The little green Pinto spent several minutes speeding around this complex before emerging once more onto a piece of straight highway.

Bognor frowned. "Aren't we going back the way we came?"

"Correct."

"Isn't that a little melodramatic?"

"Not if you're about to be charged with murder."

Bognor considered this. "I suppose not," he said. "Would you mind telling me where we're going? It would have been much simpler to have had a drink at the hotel." He was irritated.

"It won't take very long, but I need to be sure we are not followed. We have a lot to talk about and I want no interruptions. The ferry leaves in ten minutes."

"Ferry?"

"I thought we would talk in a summer cottage on Wards Island. It is not used in winter but I have borrowed the keys. Louise has been there since lunch time, warming it up. We will be quite comfortable and very private."

"Good."

They lapsed back into silence as the car headed east along Lakeshore Boulevard to the ferry terminal. There Bognor found himself hurried through turnstiles and onto one of the tall black-and-white boats he had seen from his hotel window that morning. His escort took him through heavy doors and into a long panelled saloon with wooden seats. There was nobody else on board at all, and only a minute or so after boarding there was a rattle of chains, a churning of ancient engines and the old boat reversed clumsily away from the quay and turned to move out to the island. "Good," said the man, smiling broadly. "We have given them the slip." He took off a heavy fur-lined glove and extended a bony hand with dark hairs prominent on the backs of the fingers.

"Jean-Claude Prideaux," he said. "I am sorry for what you call the melodrama, but I am afraid it is essential."

"Simon Bognor," said Bognor unnecessarily, heart missing a beat and a half. "Not the Prideaux who was Farquhar's secretary?"

Prideaux pushed back a lock of jet-black hair which had fallen across his forehead. For a moment he stared out of the window at the white-flecked waves across the harbour and the spray whipped against the glass by the wind. Then he nodded curtly, lips tight. "I was Farquhar's secretary," he said.

"I see," said Bognor, not seeing much at all but wondering if perhaps the faint glimmer at the end of the tunnel might possibly represent light. "And you think you're a prime suspect?"

"I know," said Prideaux. He took a packet of Gitanes from the folds of his heavy-duty overcoat, offered one to Bognor, who declined, and lit it from an old-fashioned, oil-filled lighter. "Those RCMP bastards told me."

"But why," asked Bognor, wincing as the old tub lurched in a sudden gust of gale, "don't they arrest you?"

He wondered if the answer to this would be the same as the one given him by Pete Smith of the Mounties. It was.

"I have a strange form of political immunity, Mr. Bognor," said Prideaux exhaling through distended nostrils with, like the fingers, more hair than was really pleasing. "In the present state of uncertainty Ottawa wants no move against the Quebecois,

guilty or not. They are afraid of creating martyrs. So for the time
being I am safe—in a manner of speaking. As soon as the political
situation is resolved I shall be arrested. Although there is always
the possibility that your friends in the RCMP will take matters
into their own hands. It has been known. There have been some
incidents, you know. Some very convenient accidents." He raised
sensitive black eyebrows to suggest the depths to which the
Mounties might stoop in order to get their man. "Fancies himself," thought Bognor, who was made uneasy by Latin looks in
men. He was made uneasy by Latin looks in women too but for
different reasons. In women they awoke desire, in men envy.

"But surely," said Bognor, "you have the same system here that
we have at home. Separation of powers and all that. The politicians can't nobble the judiciary and vice versa."

"Let's not play games, Mr. Bognor." Prideaux tossed his cigarette to the floor and extinguished it with his foot—a deft cruel
movement as if he were killing ants. Bognor filed it away in the
notebook of his mind.

"There's no society in the world which can't become a police
state when the situation demands it," said Prideaux. "You know
that as well as I do."

Bognor didn't answer. Instead he contemplated his feet. Below
them the engines changed pitch, and there was a double bump as
the boat hit something. Bognor hoped it was a landing stage and
not rock. Prideaux stood.

"This is our stop," he said, and led Bognor out into the night.
This, it seemed to him, was appreciably colder than it had been
on the mainland. He turned up the collar of his quilt, sunk his
hands deep into his pockets and wondered what Monica was
doing. Five-hour time difference. She would be asleep. Alone, he
hoped. He was sure she was eminently chaste and trustworthy
and yet always when he was abroad on missions such as this he allowed himself frissons of doubt, if only to excuse his own half-
hearted aspirations towards sexual adventure.

"It is idyllic in summer," said Prideaux as they struck out across
an open space towards a line of dim and scattered lights. "Under
threat, of course. Authority dislikes this sort of unconformist behaviour. Most of the islands are leisure park, but people actually

live here and that is untidy as far as the politicians and the bureaucrats are concerned. They want to raze it all to the ground, make it neat. A McDonald's perhaps, somewhere to buy Coke. Can you imagine?"

"Only too well." Bognor stumbled on a patch of ice, cursed loudly but did not fall. Prideaux grabbed his elbow.

"I have a torch," he said, pulling one from his pocket and shining it in front of them. The snow was patchy, but thick in places. "It's not far," said Prideaux. "Another five minutes, that's all."

"Doesn't it ever get cut off?" asked Bognor, a note of apprehension creeping into his voice. "Do the ferries run all through winter?"

"In a manner of speaking." Prideaux laughed, again without much sign of humour. "Sometimes the ice is too thick, but then you can walk across so you don't need the boat. But don't worry. Winter hasn't started yet. There's no problem."

Inwardly Bognor sighed. He was absurdly relieved when, a few minutes later, they reached a small wooden cabin with an oil lantern swinging from the roof of its veranda. As they climbed the wooden steps and then stamped the snow from their feet on the timbers in front of the door he was immensely relieved to see it open and feel a surge of warmth come bowling out like desert wind.

"Jeez," said Prideaux, pocketing the torch, "you've sure got this place steamed up."

"It's a new stove," said the little girl, "but don't just stand there letting the cold in. Hurry." They did as they were told, Prideaux stopping briefly to kiss her on both checks, Bognor shaking hands. "My name is Louise Poitou," she said.

"Poor Mr. Bognor," she said, "your hand is so cold. Come and sit by the stove. Jean-Claude will fix you a drink. I brought wine and a bottle of rye, Jean-Claude. There is ice in the freezer."

"No ice," said Bognor, struggling with his new coat, pleased at last because he was seeing his attractive little Quebecoise again so soon. He was apprehensive, absurdly, in case she was married or otherwise attached to Jean-Claude. She did not wear a wedding ring, nor he, but that meant nothing.

"Rye?" asked Prideaux from the kitchen.

He agreed to have it neat, feeling the need to revive the inner Bognor, and in a moment the three of them were all sitting in the dilapidated cane furniture raising their glasses in a toast to each other. Bognor was so shattered by his experiences that he even accepted a cigarette.

"Now," he said. "I wonder if you would mind telling me what this is all about?"

"I've made a sort of cassoulet," said Louise smiling. "Sausages and beans really but a little goose as well, and a lot of garlic, is that okay?"

"Sensational," said Bognor, meaning it, and enjoying the smile, "but I take it you have asked me here for something more than undiluted rye and Canadian cassoulet."

Jean-Claude Prideaux leaned back until his chair creaked. He breathed smoke through his nose towards the ceiling. He returned to an upright sitting position and leaned forward, fixing Bognor with an appraising Gallic stare, took a mouthful of rye, puckered his mouth, swilled the alcohol around, as if he was about to spit it out, thought better of it, swallowed and said,

"Do you have any theory?"

"About who killed Sir Roderick?"

"Of course."

"If I had, I'm afraid I would hardly be able to share it with someone who is, on his own evidence, a prime suspect."

Prideaux digested this for a moment, together with some more smoke and alcohol. Then he said, "Mr. Bognor, may I be perfectly frank?"

Bognor said he would like that very much.

"My situation is extremely delicate."

Bognor examined the palms of his hands and said nothing.

"You must understand that I am a Quebecois."

Bognor nodded.

"A Quebecois nationalist. I am committed to *la Québec libre*. I am not a friend of English Canada."

Bognor decided it was time he spoke. "Quite," he said.

"I would stop at nothing to secure the independence of my country."

"Nothing?"

Prideaux leaned even farther forward. "You are quite correct, Mr. Bognor. If it was necessary I would kill for Quebec."

"But this time it was not necessary?"

Prideaux repeated the sentence almost word for word. "This time it was not necessary."

Throughout all this the girl remained quiet, watching the two men like a spectator at a tennis match.

"This was not a political murder," she said now, softly. "Farquhar was killed by some other person, for some other reason. That is not the same as saying we would not have killed him. It makes it a difficult case to argue. Motive, opportunity, Jean-Claude had both, and, just as important, he would have had no scruples. He would not have flinched. Eh, Jean-Claude?"

"Nor you either?" Bognor glanced at her sharply, and she lowered her eyelids.

"Nor me," she agreed softly.

Bognor looked round the cabin, took in the spartan furnishings, the Emily Carr reproductions, the modern wood-burning stove, rows of enamel mugs on hooks locked into pegboard.

It took a long time to explain what their group really consisted of. It stemmed from their dislike of the Parti Québecois, which, for the time being, represented the mainstream of Quebec nationalism. They disliked the populist posturing of its leader, René Levesque, and they accused it of racism, anti-Semitism, even neofascism. They themselves were men of the left. Not very far left by European standards but far more radical than any popular political organization in Canada. Recognizing that the PQ was the most likely organization to secure independence for *la belle province* the members of the group were content to bide their time and lie low. They were known cryptically as "Seven" because that had been the cell's original strength when they had first got together as students in Quebec City's Laval University. Their only allegiance was to Quebec and to each other and their plan was to conceal their true political beliefs and infiltrate as many English-speaking and federal institutions as possible. They were, in the contemporary jargon of espionage, "sleepers" or "moles."

In the whole of Canada no individual and no organization was more strenuously Francophobe than Farquhar and Mammoncorp.

Farquhar's ambition, expressed in his characteristically pungent phrase, was to "screw those damned froggoes whenever I get the chance." For Seven it was a prime objective but it was also an impossibly hard nut to crack. Then, two years earlier, Prideaux returned from a prolonged academic perambulation around the universities of Harvard, Paris, London, Lausanne and Gabon at exactly the time that Farquhar advertised for a secretary. It seemed impossible that Farquhar with *his* prejudices would take on a Quebecker. Prideaux, however, argued that Farquhar would enjoy having a froggoe to kick around. And so it proved. Prideaux was the only Quebecois out of eighty applicants, but he got the job. He did it well too, enduring Farquhar's hectoring jibes and a whole series of petty humiliations and, biting back the slightest hint of criticism or insolence, building up a position of remarkable trust. By the time of his death Farquhar scarcely moved without Prideaux at his side. Prideaux monitored his phone calls, he supervised his entertaining, he controlled his diet, he even arranged his girls. Latterly he had even, by great stealth, begun to make inroads on Farquhar's Francophobia, convincing him, almost, that de Gaulle had been a great man (in his own way), Camembert a great cheese (if you like that sort of thing) and Château Lafite a great wine. (This last required no qualification and virtually no persuasion.) More significantly Prideaux managed to persuade him that, for example, Farquhar's bid for control of Quebec's asbestos deposits or her wood-pulp industry were inherently unsound. Or so he claimed.

This exposition lasted a full half hour, during which Bognor did not interrupt except to signify assent when little Louise offered him a second helping of rye. When Prideaux finally came to an end, Bognor said,

"So on your own admission you had a plausible political motive. You are a professional Quebec nationalist. Farquhar was Quebec's most dedicated and powerful opponent. You were also on the train when he died. The only other person on the train was Amos Littlejohn."

Prideaux shrugged. "I didn't like Farquhar. In fact I detested him. On political and personal grounds. But like I said, I was doing a good job. It made more sense for us to keep Farquhar alive and for me to go on softening him up and stopping him screwing Quebec. If he died and Cernik or Harrison Bentley took over, things would be worse. They dislike the Quebecois just as much as Farquhar and they didn't have a Quebecois secretary to improve the situation."

"True," said Bognor. "Or at least true-ish."

"And, as far as the deed itself is concerned it didn't have to be done by me or Amos. It was all in the bottle. And the bottle was sealed. He always poured his own bath oil."

"The bath oil is a problem," admitted Bognor. "I grant you that."

"The food is ready," said Louise. "Are you ready for food?"

Bognor said he was always ready for food.

They ate. The food was good.

Prideaux poured red wine from a flagon. It was from British Columbia.

"Could be worse," he said. "Not what I was accustomed to while working for Sir Roderick, but fair enough for what it is."

"Have you told him about the bath oil, Jean-Claude?" asked Louise. As she asked the question there was a crash from outside, and all three paused in their eating to look at one another enquiringly.

"Tree," said Prideaux. "There was quite a wind coming over."

"There still is quite a wind," said Louise. "Listen."

They listened. Bognor, in particular, listened with apprehension. He had been so intent on Prideaux's story that he had not noticed the weather. The house was creaking alarmingly.

"I'll just check," said Prideaux, picking up his torch from the battered pine chest where he had left it. He put on his coat and went out, letting in a great gust and having to fight to push the door open.

"Will the ferry still be running?" asked Bognor, spearing a sausage with his fork and scraping beans up with his knife.

"Oh, yes," said the girl. "The ferry never stops." She chewed on a mouthful, then took a gulp of wine. "I'm sorry to have brought you out here like this," she said, "you must be very tired." She smiled at him from under those heavy lids.

"What was it you were saying about the bath oil?"

"Oh," she took another mouthful of wine and shook her head, "Jean-Claude had better tell you," she said. "It is his story. I don't really understand it all. To tell you the truth I'm glad he's gone and I don't care who killed him."

Bognor had a mouth full of beans. When he had swallowed them he said,

"He does sound like a regular four-letter man. But on the other hand I'm not sure that's an excuse for gassing him in his bath."

"I'm sorry," she said, looking prettily perplexed. "What is a four-letter man?"

"Oh," said Bognor. "Just an expression. A bad sort. Not the sort of chap you'd go into the jungle with. Or have in the house, come to that."

She was still looking less than fully comprehending and more than just attractive when the door opened, admitting another chill gust and Prideaux, who was looking blue and snow-blown. "It *was* a tree," he said. "It just missed the Macfarlanes' deck. It's a regular blizzard out there."

He came back to the dining table and helped himself to more food and drink.

"The bath oil," said Bognor. "You were going to tell me about the bath oil."

"The murder weapon, yes." Prideaux smiled laconically. "*Mis en bouteille pour Sir R. Farquhar.*"

"Quite."

"That was altogether too much for the Mounties, you know. Quite beyond their comprehension."

"I can imagine." Bognor chewed on his beans. As a child he had been unusually fond of Mr. Heinz's beans and in the matter of beans the child had indeed proved father to the man, though nowadays it was true he preferred them with garlic and tomato and a suspicion of preserved goose.

"What they still don't realize," continued Prideaux, "is that bath oil was Sir Roderick's Christmas present this year. Everybody got a case of his own exclusive, personalized Balenciaga."

Bognor frowned. "With their own names on?"

"No, no, he was far too mean for that. To be quite frank, he'd overordered. It paid him to order in bulk and the bigger the bulk the lower the cost per bottle. He ordered several thousand. Enough bath oil to keep him going for hundreds of years."

"And so he off-loaded a few as Christmas presents?" Bognor listened to the weather pounding the little wooden house and thought of the bottle of Balenciaga he had seen in Harrison Bentley's bathroom. A Christmas present from Farquhar. No wonder he had been disliked.

"How many? And to whom?" Bognor intended to sound incisive but had a mouth half full of beans. He was also, he realized, quite suddenly, slightly drunk and extremely tired. This was no time to be conducting a cross-examination. He ought to be in bed.

"Each person got a box of twenty," said Prideaux. "I can't tell you offhand how many would have been sent them, but the list will be on file somewhere. In fact I may have it in my papers. I could let you have it tomorrow."

"Yes," said Bognor. "Yes. That would be helpful."

Louise cleared away their plates and produced some cheese, French brie and Oka, an intriguing Quebecois variety made by monks. She also put on a kettle for coffee. She had brought freshly ground beans from a new place in Hazelton Lanes. Bognor was beginning to think highly of her.

"Did you get any yourself?" he asked Jean-Claude.

"No. But I could have taken any whenever I wanted. It hardly provides me with an alibi. But it does show you that Amos and I were not the only people who might have murdered him."

"Could they have substituted their oil for his?"

"They were all known to him," said Louise. "It would have been possible, yes. For all of them."

"I see." Bognor picked at a piece of goose or other matter which had become lodged between two front teeth. The girl had even provided toothpicks, though conceivably they had been left over from summer. They had a faintly stale feel. "You never told the Mounties about the Christmas presents?"

"I told them very little."

Louise turned round from the stove. "They are pigs, really. You must understand that. If Jean-Claude had told them something like that it would only have made them more convinced that he was guilty. They would think he was trying to shift the blame, that's all."

"They wouldn't have believed him?"

She shrugged violently and made a dismissive noise, impossible to reproduce accurately on paper but most nearly rendered as "Pouf!"

"But," Bognor was indulging his old habit of thinking out loud, a ponderous process, especially at this time of night, "they could easily have found out. I mean, didn't any one of Sir Roderick's friends tell them that they'd got some of his special bath oil for Christmas?"

"They're not stupid," said Prideaux. "They all knew how the old bastard had been killed. If they let on that they were, as it were, in possession of loaded revolvers of the same calibre that fired the fatal shot then they would be automatically putting themselves under suspicion. Wouldn't they?"

"But not as much suspicion as if the Mounties found out on their own and realized that they had been concealing the evidence."

Prideaux pulled a face. "*Je m'en doute*," he said. "I don't think your friend Smith of the Mounties was ever interested in looking beyond me. The minute he realized I was from Quebec and, as you might say, politically inclined, then he decided I had done it. Sure it's circumstantial, but it's neat. Neat enough for them, at any rate."

The monks' cheese was unusual but far from unpleasant.

"You really didn't do it then?" he asked, staring hard at Sir Roderick's former secretary.

Louise answered for him. "There was no political reason for killing him," she said. "Jean-Claude had no other reason for killing. Many many others had good reason."

"She's right," said Prideaux. "Why should I kill him? It was a good job. He was an enemy, I agree, but I was educating him. Besides, he left me nothing. Everyone else has something. Even Amos has the horses. So why should I kill him?"

"Forgive me," said Bognor. "That's not the question. The question is, Did you kill him? You still haven't answered that."

There was a silence broken only by the wind beating against

the cabin, straining to blow in the doors and windows, tugging at the roof. Bognor had read about American storms, mad whirlwinds and tornadoes that struck, suddenly laying waste whole communities in seconds, corkscrewing solid stone houses into the air, flinging cars about, killing people.

"No," said Jean-Claude eventually, "I did not kill him."

Louise poured coffee and found a half-full bottle of cognac. Jean-Claude produced a packet of cheroots. Bognor accepted one and sat smoking thoughtfully, allowing fatigue and alcohol to overcome him, as he contemplated the complexities of the case. Conversation, now that the purpose of his visit was achieved, became embarrassed, stilted, desultory. All three clearly wanted to get away to think about what had been said and to ponder its effects on each other. After a while Louise rinsed the dishes under the tap. She had a rucksack into which she packed the remaining cloves of garlic and one or two cooking implements she had brought with her in the morning. It was a quarter to twelve. Last ferry for mainland left at midnight.

"Okay," said Jean-Claude. "Better hit the trail." And they went gingerly out into the storm, Jean-Claude leading the way with his torch, Bognor next and Louise bringing up the rear. Bognor felt torn between extreme tiredness, a certain amount of apprehension and a ridiculous desire to giggle. He managed to conquer the fatigue and bite back the laughter, but the fear was less easy. It was a real storm. The wind shrieked at them, threatening to blow them over, so that after a few stops Jean-Claude fell back and indicated mainly by sign and gesture that they should march on three abreast holding on to each other for support. It was snowing hard and the flakes came at them horizontally in the Canadian style to which he was becoming accustomed. Louise was now in the middle of the trio and Bognor contrived to hold on to her as tightly as possible, though her fur coat and his gloves were so thick that it was impossible to derive any real physical contact from the hug. It was in every sense quite chaste, though Bognor experienced a pang of jealousy when his right arm came into contact with Jean-Claude's left and he was reminded that he was sharing the girl with Prideaux.

They reached the landing stage five minutes before the ferry was due.

"Usually you can see the lights of the city," Jean-Claude shouted in Bognor's ear as they stood huddled in the rudimentary shelter with its two enormous life belts roped to the side. "It's not that far. Only half a mile or so."

Peering out towards the north it was impossible to see more than a few yards. The night was like soup and the lake, even though this part was as sheltered as the Solent, was churned into a froth of wave and spume.

"Do you think he'll come?" bawled Bognor, in two minds about whether or not the crossing would be worth the risk and the discomfort. He was not a brave sailor and he was inclined to queasiness. He was aware that he had eaten too much cassoulet. Beans on a high sea were a recipe for almost certain disaster.

"The ferry always comes," said Prideaux, though he too seemed to be regarding the lake with more anxiety than he was going to admit.

"It's unusual for the time of year," said Louise, shivering, and withdrawing further into her shell of fur.

They waited until midnight. And for five minutes more. And then for another five minutes. And then another five. Finally Jean-Claude looked round. "There is a light at old Manzi's house," he said. "I'll telephone from there. See what's happening. You two wait here." He stumbled off in the direction of the house. Bognor stamped his feet and waved his arms about, banging them forlornly against his chest.

"Christ," he exclaimed, "it's bloody cold."

Louise's face peered up at him out of the darkness. Little more than her eyes and nose were visible for she had a scarf and fur hat, the one pulled well up, the other well down. She giggled.

"Bloody cold," she called out, mimicking his Englishness, and then, before he could complain or remonstrate, she put her arms round him and rubbed her hands vigorously against his back, still looking up into his face and giggling mischievously. After a moment she stopped this and snuggled her head against his chest. Bognor put his arms round her and told himself very firmly that he was only trying to keep them as warm as possible in these appalling conditions. At the back of his mind there was a persistent image of Monica Bognor which, try as he would, he could not quite banish. This was, he kept telling himself, perfectly innocent. All the same he kept a keen weather eye out for the returning lantern of Jean-Claude Prideaux and when he saw it bobbing towards them through the swirling, eddying snowflakes, he disengaged himself as swiftly as he could without seeming rough. She too evidently felt a little compromised. She made no resistance and moved a few feet away from Bognor where she stood, rubbing her hands together. "Bloody, bloody cold," she said, mimicking him again, before Prideaux came within earshot. The three words made Bognor glow.

"No ferry," shouted Prideaux as he neared them. "It's cancelled. I've never heard anything like it." He stared across the lake as if willing the boat to come to them, but the air remained impenetrable, yielding up nothing. "I asked Manzi if we could borrow his launch," said Prideaux, "but he says it leaks like a sieve and he's run out of gas. I guess we'll just have to spend the night at the cottage. We have our coats and there are plenty of blankets."

Bognor experienced a number of mixed emotions on hearing this, but he was too tired to analyze them. By the time they had trudged back through the snow to the cottage, he was feeling exhausted beyond recovery. He even refused offers of more drink or coffee, and had no sooner loosened his tie, removed his shoes, and climbed under a pile of blankets and his coat than he was asleep. For once he did not dream.

CHAPTER 5

He awoke to find the sun streaming in through the windows. Louise was kneeling beside him, a hand on his shoulder, a steaming mug of coffee in her other hand.

"Hallo," she smiled. "Good morning. You are very difficult to wake, you know. You sleep like a, like a . . . Well I don't know what you sleep like, but you are very difficult to wake. And you snore a little, I am afraid."

"You're not the only person who says that." Bognor stretched. He felt a little fragile but not as bad as he had feared. He accepted the coffee and tried a tentative smile. It did not hurt so he broadened it, hoping it did not look too lopsided or louche. He wanted it to be a bright, good-morning smile, not a leer. She smiled back so that he assumed it had looked all right, even though he felt unkempt and unshaven.

"Jean-Claude has gone to Manzi to phone the ferry office," she said, rising to her feet as he took the mug. "It's a beautiful day. I don't think there will be any problem."

Bognor drank the coffee gratefully, then got up and sluiced cold water over his face. It was only just after eight o'clock. He had another coffee and went out on to the veranda. She was right. The water sparkled, flat as the snow which lay thick and crunchy on the grass in front of them. On the mainland the Toronto skyline gleamed, its gold and silver towers reflecting the dazzling sun, the CN Tower braced like a rocket before blast off. From the top of it on a day like this Bognor guessed you could see forever. He smiled. In the middle of the lagoon two stumpy black-and-white ferries churned past each other, scarcely even bobbing on the placid water.

"Nice, eh?" She came out on the deck and stood beside him,

coffee in hand, eyes narrowed against the glare. She had washed and made up and looked fresh as a snowdrop. Bognor was unhappily conscious of his dishevelled, unshaven state.

"I hope you won't be late for work," he ventured.

"Oh no," she laughed lightly. "I have a class at ten. Otherwise nothing."

"A class? What are you studying?"

"Economics. But I'm not studying, I'm supposed to be teaching it."

"Oh," Bognor was embarrassed. "I'm sorry. I didn't realize. I mean I didn't intend to imply . . ."

She put a hand momentarily on his elbow. "I'm flattered you should take me for a student," she said. She paused. "How long will you stay?"

"I don't know. As long as it takes. How long is a piece of string?"

She laughed. "You're funny," she said. "Do you think you will be able to find who killed him? It will be difficult to convince those RCMP idiots. They only believe what they want to believe."

"We're all guilty of that," said Bognor. Then, depressed by this uncharacteristically profound generalization, he said, "Perhaps you'd have dinner with me one night?"

"I'd like that," she said, watching, like him, as Jean-Claude Prideaux came out of Old Manzi's house a few hundred yards away and began to walk towards them. "But what about your wife?"

"Oh, she's miles away," said Bognor, then stopped. "Anyway, how do you know I'm married?"

She didn't answer, just laughed. Bognor coloured slightly and she must have noticed, because she said, kindly, "Of course I would like to have dinner with you," adding with a flirtatious smile, "as long as your wife really is miles away."

"Good," said Bognor. "How do I find you?"

Prideaux was approaching. Soon he would be within earshot. Bognor did not wish him to overhear this conversation.

"Call me at U. of T. Economics Faculty."

"Don't you have a home number?"

"I'm never there," she said firmly. "The university is much more reliable."

"Okay," said Bognor. "I'll call you."

Prideaux waved at him cheerily and called "Hi." Bognor waved back. Suddenly he felt pleased to be here. Although the surrealist city skyline was only a few hundreds yards away it felt like the middle of the country. Bognor was reminded of a kampong off the coast of Singapore, the time the Second Secretary had collapsed with food poisoning in the car park. He had the same odd sensation of standing in primitive rural surroundings while staring, detached, at the ultramodern city. Two worlds separated by nothing but a stretch of probably polluted water. He wondered which he preferred: standing in the city looking out at countryside or standing in the country looking in at the city. He wasn't sure. Silly sort of question to ask oneself anyway, particularly when standing here in the almost unmarked snow was so uncommonly bracing and sexy. He felt as if he were in a cigarette advertisement.

"Ferries running all right, I see," he called out to Prideaux.

"Sure," said Prideaux. "I've never heard of them missing out like last night. All drunk if you ask me. I'm sorry about it. I hope we haven't ruined your schedule."

"Don't really have a schedule," said Bognor. "Not my style." This was true. He liked to roll along gathering moss. Even when he produced plans they went astray within minutes of his making them and on the whole he preferred this. The unexpected was by definition more exciting, and even though he had endured his share of shocks and disasters, things usually panned out in the end. Besides, there was no point in knowing about disasters before they happened. That was a sure way of becoming depressed.

A few minutes later they set off for the landing stage, where a ferry duly docked and took them back to the terminal. Jean-Claude and Louise dropped him off at his hotel. They both waved as the little green Pinto shot away into the traffic. Louise smiled too.

There were two messages waiting with his keys at reception. "Mrs. Bognor called. Will you call back please." And "Mr.

Parkinson called. Will you call back please." He glanced at his watch and saw that it was just after nine. He could do with a shave, some fresh orange juice and coffee, maybe a croissant and then a kip. He smiled as he got into the elevator, which ran up and down the outside of the building and made him feel ill. He smiled through a bath and breakfast and he was still smiling when his head hit the pillow and he resigned himself to harmless adulterous dreams.

He did not, however, smile when the phone rang at eleven o'clock.

Instead, he regarded it balefully and willed it to stop. It did not.

He picked it up. "Two five two six," he said irritably.

"Mr. Bognor?" It was the girl on the switchboard. She pronounced it "Bahgner."

"Sorry. Wrong room," he said, and put down the receiver sharply.

He had just put his head back under the pillow when the phone rang again. Once more he willed it go away but it continued to shrill at him piercingly and insistently. He picked it up and was about to say "Wrong number" when his wife's voice came crackling angrily across the Atlantic.

"Simon. What on earth is going on? That was you just now."

"What do you mean 'just now?' I haven't spoken to you since" —he looked at his watch—"the day before the day before yesterday. Or thereabouts."

"Don't be ridiculous, darling, I quite distinctly heard the operator asking for you and then I heard you saying 'wrong room.' What do you mean by it?"

"She didn't ask for me. She asked for someone called 'Bahgner' or 'Bugner.' Certainly not *Bognor*."

"Don't be so childish. Where have you been?"

"Here, of course." What, he wondered, had got into Monica? Marriage obviously didn't agree with her. He decided to meet attack with attack. "Do you know what time it is?" he enquired, aggrieved. "You've woken me up."

"Honestly, darling, what is going on out there?" His wife's voice now sounded alarmingly outraged. "It is four o'clock in

London, which means that it is eleven o'clock in Toronto. Why are you asleep at eleven o'clock in the morning?"

"Jet lag," he said, deflated. A still small voice told Bognor that he was in danger of putting himself irretrievably in the wrong. And this for no good reason. He was aware that he felt a marginal guilt about having spent the night in the company of Louise Poitou and Prideaux but not because of anything that had happened. He was in the clear on that score. Well, more or less. His guilt was entirely in the mind.

"Oh, God, Monica," he said. "I *am* sorry. The fact of the matter is I got stuck on an island in the middle of *The Mousetrap.* There was a storm and the ferry didn't turn up."

There was a long pause. "That sounds like you, Simon," said Monica's voice dully. "You'd better go on."

"Not much to go on about. I had a rendezvous with this man, the prime suspect as a matter of fact, and he didn't want to be followed with anyone so he took me off to this island and, as I say, the last ferry didn't show."

I rang and rang last night," said Monica. "I rang every hour from eight o'clock your time until two in the morning."

"Oh." Bognor could not think of anything sensible to say.

"Is that all you can say?" asked Monica. Now she was beginning to sound tearful. Bognor tried desperately to think of something conciliatory.

"Not at all. It's just that, well, it was business. This chap had something to tell me so I felt I had to go and listen to him in case it was something important. As a matter of fact it was rather."

"What?"

"I'll tell you when I see you. It's not something I think I ought to discuss on the phone."

"That's what I wanted to talk to you about."

"No," said Bognor. "I'd rather not. Not on the phone."

"Not that, silly. When I see you. That's what I meant. I spoke to Parkinson and he says you may be out there for weeks. Uncle Freddie's legacy just came through. It's five thousand, would you believe. So I thought I'd hop out and we could have a bit of a delayed honeymoon."

"Oh." Dammit, thought Bognor, I must try to sound enthusiastic. "Did Parkinson really say I'd be here for weeks?" he asked.

"Yes."

"Well, I do wish he wouldn't say things like that when he has no idea what's going on at ground level. I may be back in days."

"Oh." It was her turn for the drab, wet little word.

"Look"—Bognor pulled himself together—"it would be wonderful to have you out here. It's just that, quite frankly, things are hellishly complicated. There's a political element which I don't think Parkinson has appreciated. I'd love to see you, but I'd rather you didn't come until you've cleared it with Parkinson, after I've spoken to him. All right?"

"All right."

"How are you otherwise?" he asked solicitously.

"I'm fine. I was worried though."

"Well, you mustn't worry."

"Why not? You're such a fool."

"That's not a very nice thing to say."

"True, though."

"Yes. Well. Maybe. No. Hell. Not at all. Look this is costing an awful lot. Let's talk later. Maybe I'll see you soon. Must rush. 'Bye."

" 'Bye."

Click. Married life, thought Bognor, is by no means a bed of roses. He decided to snatch another hour's sleep and settled back under the bedclothes feeling somewhat troubled. He began to dream. But just as he began to dream glorious Technicolor dreams he was disturbed again. Once more the phone. He looked at his watch. Eleven-thirty. He glared at the telephone, then seized it as if by snatching at it and squeezing hard he might succeed in throttling the thing.

"Bognor," he rasped.

"Simon?" The voice sounded slightly tremulous, unsure of itself.

"Yes," he said, hoping it was who he thought it was.

"It is Louise."

"Oh. Hello."

"Can you come skiing this afternoon?"

"Skiing?" Bognor's hands began to sweat. "I don't know that I have the gear."

"You can borrow some trousers and an anorak from Jean-Claude. Skis and boots you can hire at the zoo."

"The zoo?"

"Yes. We are going skiing at the zoo."

"Listen, Louise, is this some kind of a joke?"

That irresistible tinkling laugh. "I am an assistant professor of economics. I don't joke. Listen. It's important. There is a girl-friend of mine I want you to meet."

"But couldn't we meet here? Or at your place? Skiing really isn't my sort of thing."

"It's cross-country skiing. No problem. And I promise you it is connected with the Farquhar murder. It may help to prove to you that Jean-Claude is innocent."

"I still don't see why it's necessary to go skiing to meet her."

"Don't argue." She giggled again. "I'll come by the hotel and pick you up at twelve-thirty. We can have lunch out there."

Click.

Oh, God, thought Bognor, I'm too old for this. He retreated under the bedclothes to see if he could spend ten minutes in con-templation of the problems which beset him. It seemed to him that these were increasing with every phone call. The thought of skiing, even with the delectable Miss Poitou, appalled him. He had never been much of a games player and he was now hopelessly out of condition. He told himself that he was not very overweight and could manage a game of tennis without undue fa-tigue. Or a length or two of the swimming pool. But skiing was something else. A different sort of muscle altogether and not one he had used in years. Not since Wengen in '63 when he had pulled his Achilles tendon and come down the Lauberhorn on a ski-borne stretcher. It might not have been the Lauberhorn, actu-ally, but that was what he told people and he had come to believe it. The prospect of being with Louise Poitou was attractive but dampened by the phone call from his beloved in London. And then there was the Farquhar murder. Did Prideaux do it? If Har-rison Bentley was a recipient of personalized bath oil might not he have done the deed? Or anyone else, come to that. He was not much further on, though he very much resented the attitude of Smith of the Mounties and if only for that reason was disposed to believe in Prideaux's innocence. Insufficient motive. Besides, he was too obvious a suspect. Private secretaries had too many opportunities for murdering the boss. To succumb to them would be foolhardy. No, he was inclined to rule out Prideaux. He disliked Harrison Bentley even more. Besides, there were others: the Cerniks and La Bandanna Rose. They were bound to have had Balenciaga for Christmas. It was like being caught up in an absurd distortion of last night's Christie play. One Detective. One Corpse. A fistful of suspects each one with a smoking gun. He burrowed still farther under the bedclothes, then emerged with a dramatic spring onto the carpet. Skiing involved thigh muscles. He essayed a full-knees bend and toppled over, pushed himself back into the squat position and attempted to rise to attention slowly and gracefully as he had been taught at school. He experienced a creaking sensation and heard a couple of sharp snaps which, oddly enough, caused him no pain. Once he was upright he stood on his toes. This was gratifyingly easy. He then lowered himself slowly, finding it simple at first but having to hurry the final furlong and falling again at the end. There were a couple more sharp cracks on the way. He sat on the carpet dejectedly and wondered whether to try a toe touch. He did and ended up six inches short of the target. With a superhuman final effort he managed to brush his feet with the very tip of an index finger. This was not good. Louise would laugh at him. He smiled. The idea did not displease him. After all, he was old enough to be her uncle.

He subsided onto the bed and reached for the phone. "I want a London number," he said to the courteous girl who wished him good day.

"London, England?"

"Yes. London, England." It disturbed him to be in a country where such a question could be asked with apparent seriousness. He gave the girl Parkinson's home number and was rewarded seconds later with a series of electronic blips followed by Parkinson's bark. More of a yap than a bark, he thought, at least from a distance of three and a half thousand miles.

"Parkinson," yapped Parkinson.

"Bognor, here. It's a very sensitive business this," he said. "I'm not at all happy about it."

"None of us are happy about it, Bognor. We're not paid to be happy. We're paid to get on with the job. And we knew it was a sensitive business as soon as you became involved in it. The most mundane and straightforward little murder becomes an international incident as soon as your elephantine presence makes itself felt."

"I think it might be as well for me to come home quite soon," said Bognor. "It seems to me that the RCMP have got it wrapped up. At least they're convinced they've got it wrapped up and I don't fancy another argy-bargy with the Mounties. Not on their home turf."

One of Parkinson's menacing silences ensued. Somehow he managed to send the threat along the wires so that for a moment Bognor felt as if he were sitting in Parkinson's office trying to focus on that dreadful black-and-white photograph of Her Gracious Majesty above the Parkinson head while the Parkinson stare drilled remorselessly into him, accompanied perhaps by a quiet persistent drumming of exasperated fingers on the mahogany surface of his regulation senior civil servant's desk. There was no such photograph in his hotel room here in Toronto and so he gazed out of the window at the still bright day and tried not to squirm. Then Parkinson said, "Your orders were to maintain a scrupulously low profile. And above all not to provoke a row between us and the Canadians. I told you the Minister is particularly anxious to be nice to the Canadians. The Canadians are prone to misconceived feelings of inferiority. They do not like to be patronized. Particularly by us. Do not let me hear that you are patronizing Canadians, Bognor."

"No."

"Nor disagreeing with the Royal Canadian Mounted Police."

"No."

"Which is one of the world's finest police forces."

"Which is indeed one of the world's finest police forces."

"So let us have no more loose talk about returning imminently."

"No. Well. Not unless circumstances demand it."

"Correction. Not unless *I* demand it."

"Same thing," said Bognor with asperity.

"As long as that is understood," said Parkinson. "Your wife sounded very distressed. She is evidently as dubious about your talent for this kind of work as I am myself. But unlike me, Bognor, she cares. I think you should remember that before you spend all night on the town again."

"I was following up a lead."

"Yes. So she said. And I would be extremely surprised if the so-called lead led anywhere at all. Mmm?"

"I wouldn't put it as strongly as that."

"No, you wouldn't. You never do. In any case I told Mrs. Bognor that if she was able to find the fare, as I understand she can, then the board would not be averse to taking a generous view of whatever expenses you care to submit. Do I make myself plain?"

"Very."

"And, Bognor . . ."

"Yes?"

"Please try to remember that your presence in Canada is largely cosmetic. There is very little need for you to actually *do* anything. *That* you can leave to the experts. I just want you to do what our transatlantic friends call 'hang in there.' Unruffle any ruffled feathers. Report back if our interests appear to be threatened. Don't get into trouble."

"I won't. As a matter of fact, I'm going skiing this afternoon."

"Excellent. Should you happen to do yourself an injury kindly do not use it as an excuse to return home. A hospital bed may well be the best place for you to maintain the sort of unobtrusive presence I'm looking for."

"Thank you very much."

"Not at all. When Mrs. Bognor arrives I suggest you take *her* skiing. I understand there is fine skiing somewhere called Banff."

"That's in Scotland."

"I think not," said Parkinson. "Try to be sensible until your wife arrives to look after you. I have a great deal of confidence in that young woman."

"Which is more than you have in me."

"You said it, Bognor."

"Yes," said Bognor, "and you meant it."

"Come, come." Parkinson sounded quite affable. "The transatlantic telephone is no place for such badinage. I'll wish you good skiing."

"Huh." Bognor replaced the telephone and got dressed, taking care to wear a pair of warm RAF surplus long johns next to the skin. A present from Monica. Then he went downstairs and had a hair of the dog in the shape of a Bloody Mary before going out to meet Louise.

CHAPTER 6

She arrived at the appointed hour, in a large vulgar white automobile with TRANS AM written on the back. The car was covered in wavy blue hieroglyphs not unlike the sort of illustration you used to find on canal barges. Louise was in the passenger seat beside the driver, who was a ravishing ash blonde in tight ski pants and a pink angora sweater. Bognor got in the back.

"Simon," said Louise, "this is Maggie Fox."

"Hi, Si," said Maggie, craning her neck to stare into his eyes with her own, which were a flashing Mediterranean blue. She held out a hand, heavily painted and much bejewelled. Bognor shook it, though he toyed with the idea of kissing it, which he might have done, if that had been his style. She had perfect teeth and a large heavily lipsticked mouth. About thirty, he supposed. The sort of woman who drove a certain sort of man to distraction but a little too obvious for him. Too rich, too. He found such flaunted wealth distracting.

"How was your class?" he asked, as Maggie let the car move out into the traffic. This was not the sort of machine one drove. It looked after itself. Maggie did not appear to do more than give the wheel the faintest nudge, and as far as Bognor could see there were no gears. He hoped there were brakes.

"Oh, fine," said Louise. "Did you have a good morning?"

"Yes. I talked to London."

"Good."

The car's engine, though clearly many hundreds of horsepower strong, was as silent as a Rolls-Royce, but Maggie compensated by playing a Liza Minnelli tape very loudly, snapping her fingers in time to the beat. This made conversation difficult and so Bognor was content to settle back into the upholstery and watch the city pass. They were moving north up Yonge Street, the hundred-mile-or-more straight highway which bisects the city before heading out towards the summer cottage country to the west of Georgian Bay. Presently garish neon shopfronts gave way to private houses which became more and more bungaloid and suburban as they rolled smoothly north. At length they reached the 401, and turned east towards Kingston and Montreal. After another twenty minutes of creaming along to the strains of Minnelli and then Anne Murray they reached a turning which indicated Metro Toronto Zoo.

"Did you say you were a keen skier?" asked Louise, turning to grin impishly at him.

"I'm not even a skier," said Bognor.

"We'll soon get you going," she said. "It's easy. Not like downhill."

The girls' skis were strapped to the top of the car and after they had parked as near to the main entrance as possible they pulled on anoraks and took the long narrow fiber-glass skis down and set them on the ground. Louise handed Bognor an anorak and a pair of loose windproof trousers which she said he could slip over his sweater and corduroys. Considering Jean-Claude was a good two inches taller and about four inches slimmer, they were a surprisingly good fit. He felt a little like Michelin man but he was assured by Louise and Maggie that he looked just fine.

"What's this all in aid of?" he hissed at Louise as Maggie set off ahead of them. She had a wonderfully athletic bottom but still Bognor could not bring himself to be attracted to her.

"Wait and see," said Louise. "Maggie is extraordinary. She collects rich men. Her husband is Johnny Baker."

"Johnny Baker?"

"You know. Johnny Baker. *The* Johnny Baker."

"Who's he?"

"Are you pulling my leg?" She looked at him, eyes wide with wonder.

"No. I've never heard of Johnny Baker."

"But everybody has heard of Johnny Baker."

"Not where I come from," said Bognor flatly.

"He's the next leader of the Liberal party bar two, and rich. Boy is he rich!"

"Rich as Farquhar?"

"Mmm. Well, I don't know. I don't suppose anybody knows for certain. He will be though. He's only just forty."

"And where does his money come from?"

"I don't like him very much," said Louise. "His early money he made from gambling and syndicates in harness racing. Maybe not criminal but too near to criminal. Now he is ultrarespectable. He has Pactolus Mines, Haute Cuisine Foods, Bonanza Banking Corporation."

"Does he have something to do with the murder?"

"I think maybe. But we'll find out when you listen to what Maggie tells you. She is a nice girl really. You mustn't be put off by how she looks."

"What makes you think I am?"

She looked up at him and smiled. "I notice certain things," she said. "You think I'm stupid?"

"No," said Bognor, "certainly not."

The heavy snowfall and the fine weather had brought out a crowd of winter sportsmen. There was a queue at the turnstile and on a high ridge to their right Bognor could see a crocodile of skiers in gay costumes, striding gracefully along the skyline pausing occasionally to swoop down a hill or climb in an economical herringbone up the next. Inside the entrance the girls bent down to strap on the skis, which fastened with a simple clamp on the toe, leaving the heel free to move up and down as you sped across the countryside.

"Okay, Si," said Maggie, patting him on the shoulder with good natured enthusiasm. "Let's get you kitted out, then you can show us a thing or two. You guys in Britain invented skiing. Know that?"

"Before my time," said Bognor.

"Aw," exclaimed the blonde. "You've got a reputation to live up to, Si."

They slid over to a hut surrounded by a forest of skis and a mountain of boots. In a trice Bognor was standing on long tapering red objects, holding himself upright on poles secured by tapes through which he had thrust his mitts. Gingerly he slid first one, then another up and down on the snow covered ground. It seemed to him that they moved with uncomfortable ease. He only hoped that the spiked poles would prevent too much ignominy.

"Okay?" asked Maggie.

"Okay?" asked Louise.

He nodded grimly. "Fine," he said. "Let's go."

It started badly for there was a steep slope at first, immediately before a long flat haul to the camel enclosure. He fell slowly, ponderously and painfully but he was able to drag up the recovery procedure from some forgotten recess of his mind and was on his feet without having to be hauled up by either of the girls. They looked horribly accomplished.

"Like this," said Maggie, lunging forward and digging a pole into the snow. Left, right, left, right, she covered the snow like a marathon runner, eating up the distance with enviable grace. After twenty yards she stopped, swivelled and called out to Bognor to follow suit.

"Go on," whispered Louise at his elbow. "For Britain." She laughed.

It was a struggle and he could sense that there were some unexpected muscles in the upper leg which were being called into play after decades of disuse. He would pay for this.

At the camel house a ragged dromedary stared superciliously out at them, dribbling his disdain. They turned right past tigers, leopards, wallabies and then reindeer. Bognor wondered if he might not be getting the hang of it as he came to the reindeer. He had seen a film once about Nordic armies dressed entirely in white who skimmed about Scandinavia at astonishing speed, and for a moment he saw himself as a Flying Finn, a momentary illusion which led almost immediately to his second crash. This time Louise gave him a hand to help him up and he slipped over again as he took it, almost pulling her down with him.

"We can't talk like this," he said plaintively. "It's all I can do to stay upright."

"We'll talk at lunch," she said. "You're doing very well."

He fell several times before lunch, which, by now, had postponed itself into something more like tea. But by the time they had passed the polar bears and the beaver, busy building an intricate dam for winter, he was beginning to come to terms with it and was learning to swing his hips in a passable imitation of the girls and the many other expert skiers who passed them as they moved slowly round the course. Finally, after a long haul of uphill herringbone through a wood, they arrived at a McDonald's hamburger restaurant where, thankfully, he was able to unclip his skis and return to the relative safety of his own two feet.

"Big Mac?" asked Louise. "Hot chocolate?"

Bognor nodded and made to get them, but Louise motioned him to sit at a table outside. "I'll get them," she said. "You two have things to talk about."

Bognor expostulated mildly, then sat down opposite Maggie, who favoured him with one of her dazzling if glacial smiles.

"I hope you don't mind our meeting like this," she said. "It's just that I don't want anyone to know that I've been talking to you so I guess that ruled out my apartment or your hotel and most other places around town. Any case, you're seeing a little of how we live out here, eh?"

"Yes," said Bognor. "Very unusual."

"I adore it," she said. "Just magic. I came out here almost every day last winter." She paused. "Si," she said, in a different and self-consciously serious voice, an octave or two lower and rather husky, "You don't mind my calling you Si?"

"Not in the least," said Bognor, who did, actually, but was too well-mannered to say so.

"That's great," she said. "Only some Brits get uptight about that kind of thing. Listen, Si, may I be absolutely, perfectly frank with you?"

Bognor said he'd like that very much.

"Okay. Terrific." She took a deep breath. "I don't want to shock you, Si," she said, "but, well, not to put too fine a point on it, I no longer find my husband very attractive. In bed." Bognor swallowed. "I'm not embarrassing you, am I, Si?" she asked, flashing another of her on-off smiles. "Louise told me you're a man of the world but my experience is that some Brits are sort of uptight when it comes to talking about what goes on between a man and a woman when they're in the sack together. That sort of thing doesn't shock you, does it, Si?"

"Not at all," said Bognor who never, ever, on a point of principle, discussed human biology in any but the most evasive and elliptical terms.

"So for the last year or so I've been sort of screwing around a little." Bognor winced. "Nothing, you know, dramatic. I've been very discreet because I don't want to upset my husband, but a girl only has one life, and frankly I don't believe in wasting it on a man who can't even . . ." She fluttered her eyelashes at him and smiled a little less frantically. "He was just fine when we were first married but he got bored with it. I mean, to be honest with you, Si, he is simply unable to function as a man. Forty years old and he is just totally unable to function. Can you imagine what that does to a woman? Can you imagine?"

Bognor nodded sympathetically.

"Well," she continued. "To cut a long story short, I started dating Sir Roderick Farquhar."

"You what?"

Bognor had not been expecting this.

"Well, I guess maybe 'dating' isn't exactly the right description. I mean, we were so discreet you wouldn't believe. We never, but never, went to any public place together. There was no way anyone knew what was really happening."

"And he *was* able to, as it were, 'function'?"

She shot him a mock-surprised, almost shocked glance from under pseudo-demure half-closed lids. "You British," she exclaimed, "can be just awful. But no, you guessed. For a man of his age he functioned just beautifully." She closed her eyes and shook her head. "Just beautifully," she repeated. "However"—and here she became brisk—"there was no way it was, like you know, leading anywhere. I was determined to hang on to my marriage. My motto has always been 'love 'em and leave 'em,' kiddo. Know what I mean?"

"Even with Sir Roderick?"

"No kidding. Trouble was, he started to get really heavy, so just when I was ready to move on somewhere else he was starting to

talk to me about becoming the fifth Lady Farquhar. Or the sixth.
Or some such. Well, like I mean, 'no way.'"

Louise returned with a tray of burgers and hot chocolates.

"I'm sorry," she said. "Quite a line-up. You two okay?"

"Having a ball," said Maggie. "I was just telling him how
Farquhar suddenly came on strong·and tried to persuade me to
ditch Johnny and move in with him."

Louise nodded.

"Anyway," Maggie crammed Big Mac into her mouth and
sliced through it in one snap of her perfect teeth. "Roddie said,
'Either you move in with me and dump that arsehole of a husband, or I send him your letters.'"

"Letters?" muttered Bognor, through hamburger. "What letters?"

"Oh, you know. Like 'Roddie, darling, you were terrific. See
you Friday, your place. Mags.'"

"Cryptic rather than gushing, but still incriminating."

"Guess so. So I said, 'Don't you try to blackmail me, you bum,
I never want to see you again so long as I live, so help me God.'
And he put all the letters in a big brown envelope and sent them
straight round to Johnny."

"And Johnny? I mean your husband."

"He just went berserk," said Maggie. "Just like he was crazy.
Hit me about, and then he locked me in my room for forty-eight
hours. And he made me swear I'd never be unfaithful to him
again, or he'd kill me. And he swore he'd kill Roddie if he got the
chance."

"Kill him?"

"Oh, sure. He would, too. To be honest, I think he did, but
you're going to have one hell of a job proving it."

"When did all this happen?"

"He got the letters about a week before Roddie was rubbed
out. He hated Roddie's guts anyway. It was mutual."

Louise broke in. "That's no secret. All Bay Street knows there's
no love lost between Baker and Farquhar. That doesn't mean
they'd have killed each other. Not without Maggie providing that
extra motive. The straw that broke the camel's back, eh?"

Maggie grimaced. "Thanks a bunch, doll," she said.

Bognor sighed. "It's all very difficult," he said. "You're telling me that your husband was cuckolded by Farquhar and possibly—probably—killed him as a result."

"Yeah."

"It's a clearer motive than Jean-Claude's," said Louise.

"I suppose so." Bognor rubbed his jaw. He was beginning to think that the Mounties were wise to stay with their first suspect. "Can we walk back from here?" he asked. "I think I've had .enough skiing for today."

There was a chorus of dissent—smiles, pouts, taunts—so that despite his fatigue and his fear of skiing he felt obliged to agree. They were, it transpired, only halfway round the course, which made a circuit of the entire zoo.

The next half took them away from the animal houses towards the "Canadian domain," where wolves and bears and bison took on the climate without benefit of central heating. It was considered more difficult skiing than the first half, but the girls evidently regarded their English visitor as a challenge and were determined that he should circumnavigate the zoo no matter what. Because it was more difficult it was also less crowded. It was also getting late so that as they slithered away past the seal ponds on their way out to the wilderness there was no one to be seen ahead. There was no one immediately behind them either but about two minutes after they left, a trio of hard-looking men with the build of lumberjacks and the athleticism of hockey players skied out of the restaurant area and moved after them. They had been with them in the car park, camouflaged by the crowds, and they had remained in sight though not earshot ever since.

About a mile from lunch, Bognor and the girls paused for breath and to admire the view. The ground, covered in deep snow, fell away sharply to their right, down through forest to the river, which wound around the zoo's perimeter. The snow clung frozen to the branches and though the brightness was fading the sky was still light blue.

"Beautiful," said Bognor, shading his eyes.

"Magic," said Maggie, "and so quiet. Not another soul in sight."

"Except those guys!" exclaimed Louise, glancing back over her shoulder.

All three turned to look. The three men had also stopped about half a mile behind. They were grouped together, apparently in consultation. They had a pair of binoculars which were being passed from hand to hand.

"What do you make of that?" asked Louise quietly.

"Three men looking for bison. Or musk-ox. Or whatever you have round here," said Bognor flippantly.

"They've found what they're looking for," said Louise. "They're looking for us."

"Jeez, Louise," said Maggie. "Are you sure? Who in the world would come out here looking for us?"

"Someone who followed us," said Louise, "that's who."

"You could be right." Bognor gazed back at the men. There was absolutely nobody else in sight. The zoo had apparently emptied. It was silent too. In the distance a wolf howled, its cry taken up by another. Behind them the three men finished their deliberations and fanned out.

"Oh, my God!" said Maggie. "We've got to move, and fast."

Although the men were almost a thousand yards behind they were between Bognor and the girls and the main zoo buildings. Normally they would have skied on around three sides of a square, the third side of which took them back to the main exit. At this moment their pursuers were boxing them into the far corner of this square, a corner from which there was no escape except down the steep wooded slope and across the river. Beyond that the nearest road was God knows how far away.

There was nothing, on the face of it, to prove that the three men were giving chase, and yet Bognor, who had been chased too often to make mistakes about it, knew for certain that the men were after him. It was a reaction based on animal instinct rather than intellect. A moment before he really had thought they could be harmless seekers after bison or musk-ox, but as they lengthened their strides and moved towards them with a horrid sense of purpose Bognor experienced an old familiar fear. "Here we go again," he thought to himself, pathetically. Why did it always have to be him?

"Come on! Go!" screamed Maggie, and without another glance she lunged into racing rhythm and streaked off across the snow, leaving Louise and Bognor behind.

"I haven't a hope," said Bognor. "There's no way I can get past those monkeys. Look!" It was clear the men could ski. They were coming on in powerful graceful strides, heading straight for them. They made no effort, however, to cut off the fleeing Maggie, who seemed to have the legs of them.

"You must try to get away!" Louise shouted.

"I'll try," said Bognor. "But you go ahead! Hurry before it's too late! Get help."

"I can't leave you like this," she said. "It's terrible."

"Don't worry," he said. "They can't touch me. I'm an official representative of Her Majesty's Government. Besides, I'm armed." This last was not strictly true, but he was determined that the girl should escape and she only had seconds left. She hesitated a moment longer.

"Don't be ridiculous," he shouted. "Hurry! I'll be all right!" And then she too swung her hips, dug her ski sticks into the ground and raced away from him. One of the pursuers turned to cut her off but she was travelling too fast. To Bognor it seemed that his efforts were half-hearted and after only a few strides he turned back to join his colleagues, who were converging rapidly on Bognor. For a moment he toyed with the idea of trying to break out past them but the gap was well and truly closed by now and he was so inexpert on his skis that the exercise would be pointless. If he removed his skis and made for the ravine he would at least be equallizing the odds. It was too steep even for experienced Canadian skiers, and the trees were too close together. It would be three against one but at least it would be feet against feet and he still had a start of two or three hundred yards. He knelt down as quickly as he could and released the clip which fitted over the lip at the toe of his boots. He hesitated over the sticks but decided to hang on to one, partly for self-defence, partly to steady himself on the near-vertical side of the ravine. They were obviously confident, for as he set off on his break for freedom they scarcely increased their pace at all. He had only fifty or so yards to run but the snow was deeper than he had realized.

By the time he had gained the woods they were less than a hundred yards behind and he was almost exhausted. His breath came in short wheezing gasps and his legs were like Plasticine. The best bet, he decided, was to sit down and slide, using the trees as brakes wherever possible, and so he sat, prayed and pushed off. It was not comfortable. Within seconds the snow had penetrated his trousers so that his bottom and upper legs were saturated and freezing. Every yard he hit a tree and had to fend it off with his hands. He could not look behind and had no idea what was happening to the pursuit but when he reached the bottom he was able to turn quickly and peer upwards. He could hear a body or bodies crashing about, but he could see nothing. There was no future in waiting and so he turned to his left and began to run along the riverbank.

If he kept going along this he would come out at the zoo gates. But it would be at least two miles. He had no confidence that he could get that far on foot, much less outstrip the men in pursuit. Nevertheless they did not seem to be gaining. The crashes which he had heard earlier had died away. He stopped, and listened, quite breathless. All he could hear was the exaggerated beat of his heart against ribs, the blood pounding in his ears, evidence of his age and indolence and greed. He could see very little, either, beyond alarming little yellow sparks which, he feared, came from within rather than without. He sighed very deeply and hung his head between his knees in a futile effort to recapture his breath. No sooner had he done so than he felt a sudden explosive blow on the back of his head. For a second he remained still, then slowly keeled over, his head coming to rest in a shallow drift of snow which failed, though invigorating, to bring him out of the deep unconsciousness which now overcame him.

CHAPTER 7

He woke to find himself in darkness, trussed hand and foot like a battery fowl, and in a confined space. A very confined space. He was being shaken about. Most of the time the shaking was a constant rattle so that he felt rather as he imagined dice would feel before being cast. Occasionally there would be a more dramatic lurch and he would be thrown against the side of his container, which was metal, angular and sometimes sharp. Once or twice he had left metal objects in his trouser pockets and heard them crashing about in the washing machine or spin drier where Monica had put them without checking to see that they were there. That's what this was like. His head, particularly the back of it, was throbbing and sore and every time he was bumped his head hurt more, so that he wanted to cry out. This luxury, however, was denied him for he had some cloth stuffed in his mouth which prevented shouting, screaming or even speech. Not that speech would have been much use since he appeared to be on his own in this constricting prison. The cloth also made his mouth very dry so that he wanted to vomit. And there was a smell of oil and petrol which made this desire still stronger.

"Oh, God," he said to himself as his thoughts began to arrange themselves into something approaching order. "I'm in a car. We're going somewhere." He had never been tied up and dumped in the boot of a car before. It was not a form of travel he would recommend. Also, he feared the precedents were not good. In his experience it was a prelude to the final unpleasantness. People conveyed about the place in the boots of cars ended up as bodies. Sometimes, he knew, they were "deposited on waste ground." Sometimes they were just left in the car where they were discovered, alas too late, after an anonymous tip-off to the local police. He was quite used to being knocked unconscious by unexpected blows to the back of the head. Indeed he regarded it, very nearly, as part of his day's work. He was also quite used to great discomfort and even very great fear. But death was a new experience and not one for which he felt yet prepared.

Gingerly he tried to move his feet, but they were tied much too fast. His hands likewise. He had read and seen that in circumstances such as this people manoeuvred themselves so that their bonds came up against some sharp metallic surface. By dint of feverish rubbing the bonds were severed and as soon as the door of the boot was opened the hero, or person previously bound and gagged, leaped out confounding his captors with lightning lefts and rights or karate blows. Such, however, was not Bognor's style. There had once been attempts to teach him the rudiments of unarmed combat but these had been abandoned when it became clear that he was far more likely to damage himself than anybody else. He could feel endless sharp surfaces but there was no way in which he could use them to cut the rope at his wrists. He wondered if they were going to shoot him or just leave him to starve or suffocate. And if so why? Who were these people? Not Mounties surely? For all the vilification heaped on them and for all his own less intemperate reservations he could not believe that the RCMP would abduct and kill an official emissary of the British Board of Trade. Especially since he was here at their own invitation. Sort of. If not Mounties then it was presumably someone who was apprehensive about his investigations into the Farquhar murder. Harrison Bentley? Would that fastidious ersatz English gentleman hire brutish assassins like this? Quite possibly. Or Prideaux? Was this a hit squad from the Group of Seven or whatever his shadowy band of Quebecois extremists were called? But if so why? Prideaux was already almost convicted by the Mounties and Bognor was a potential ally, a straw, at least for Prideaux to clutch at. Indeed Bognor was under the impression that he had *been* clutched at. Which ruled out Prideaux. At least for the time being. Unless something had gone wrong since the two had parted. And then surely Louise would have said so. Or maybe she deliberately led him into a trap? Or Maggie? He hadn't cared for the pneumatic Maggie, but she *had* just confessed the secrets of her sex life to him. That was an unlikely prelude to having him kidnapped. Ouch! A more than usually violent jolt brought his ear into contact with a protruding knob. He felt tears start to his eyes. The pain was appalling. He would probably go deaf. Perhaps Amos Littlejohn was at the bottom of it. But how would he know to come looking for him on the ski piste of the Metro Zoo? The same applied to the Cerniks and La Bandanna Rose. Unless, of course, they had had a tail on him and followed the three of them from the hotel. That was possible. But wasn't it a somewhat extreme reaction? He had not even got round to questioning any of the last few suspects yet. He did not fool himself that his forensic reputation would lead any of them into such a dastardly preemptive strike. Unless of course they were in a state of real panic. Which was possible. He wished to heaven he could make a list, but there was no pencil or paper to hand. Another bad bump. His nose this time. Blood? Something warm and wet. It trickled through or past his gag and into his mouth. Blood all right. He should never have come here. He couldn't even stretch out, it was so cramped. Another lurch, even more vicious, and then, merciful heaven, it stopped. No more noise. No more bumping. Perhaps this was the end. Perhaps this was death. But no, the pain was still there. He lay still, feeling the blood trickling into his mouth. His back itched and he had an agonizing need to scratch it. Another impossibility. From outside he could hear a slamming of doors and then the crunch of footsteps on gravel. Seconds later the lid of his coffin swung up and he saw faces looking down at him. It was dark now but there were artificial lights on somewhere and he could make out the outlines of the faces though not their details. They looked big-boned, strong, stupid, just what you would expect from hired heavies.

"He still alive?" enquired one.

"Sure," replied another. "I just gave him a little tap."

"What do we do with him now?"

"Better find out. Ask the boss."

"And leave him there?"

"Sure."

"Shall I shut him up again?"

"No, just leave him. Boss may wanna talk with him."

Suddenly one of the men put a huge hand down, grabbed hold of Bognor's hair and yanked his head up. Bognor groaned. For a second the man held him there while Bognor kept his eyes tight shut, then he let go and Bognor crashed back onto the floor with another painful thud. He heard the men laugh, then turn away and crunch across the gravel.

He must have lain there for another ten minutes, maybe longer because he lost consciousness again and did not come round until the men returned. Roughly they lifted him out of the car and half carried, half dragged him through a front door which looked to Bognor much like Harrison Bentley's. Inside the house was as big, but different, more North American. Whoever it belonged to was clearly not trying to pretend to be an English gentleman. He was dragged along the hall, then left down a corridor and into a long study or office. At one end there was a massive modern desk made of steel and glass and maple wood. Behind it there was a Canadian national flag which reminded Bognor of the patriotic symbolism in Parkinson's office. All around the walls were photographs and scrolls and citations. All the latter were inscribed to the Honourable John C. Baker. The photographs were of a man shaking hands with different people, some of whom Bognor recognized, but all of whom, he guessed, were famous somewhere. The same man was sitting behind the desk but he had not bothered to put on the insincerely rapturous smile which split his face in the photographs. Instead he wore a malevolent frown which looked as if it came a great deal more naturally to him. In his mouth was a large cigar, half smoked and dead. It remained in the mouth, as if clamped, when he spoke.

"Put the guy down," he said. "No. Wait. He's filthy dirty. He'll soil the chair. Get some newspaper."

One of his captors went outside while Bognor remained, held more or less upright in the hands of the other two. They grasped him painfully tight. The Honourable John C. Baker glared at him from eyes like slits.

"You're gonna regret this, feller," he said, still not removing his cigar. Bognor grunted at him defiantly, unable to articulate real words because of his gag. This was just as well since he could think of nothing effective to say.

The third man returned with a copy of the Toronto *Star*. Baker removed the cigar and waved it at the chair in front of the desk. "Spread it over that," he said, "then put him down. And take that thing out of his mouth." The newspaper was duly laid out over the upholstery, Bognor was dropped on top of it and his gag was removed. His hands and feet, however, remained tied.

"Okay," said Baker. He nodded to his employees. "You guys split now. Have a beer in the TV room and don't leave. I'll call you later."

As they left, Baker stood and went to a cupboard set into the wall from which he removed a bottle of Chivas Regal scotch whisky and a single glass which he half filled with ice from a small freezer. Putting the glass on the desk top he filled it two thirds full of scotch, removed the cigar from his mouth, drank back half the contents of the glass, and refilled it. He then replaced the cigar, sat down again, and favoured Bognor with a long, searching and very menacing stare. Bognor consoled himself with the thought that the man was impotent. He didn't look like someone who was "unable to function as a man" but then Bognor did not know how to judge such things from purely external superficial evidence. He certainly looked like a man who drank and ate too much. His neck bulged over his collar and his gut bulged over his trouser top.

"Could I have a glass of water?" enquired Bognor with what he considered an appropriately deferential smile.

"Don't patronise me," snapped Baker, his cigar shaking. He took another slug of whisky, then attempted to light his cigar from the massive silver device on his desk.

"Where'd you get that goddamn affected accent from?" asked Baker. "You some sort of fairy?"

"Certainly not."

"British then?"

"Yes, actually."

"Jesus," Baker gulped back smoke. "First Farquhar, now some goddamn British fairy."

"I beg your pardon."

Baker stabbed at him with his cigar. "Don't you give me that, you fag," he shouted. Bognor noticed a thin dribble of saliva com-

ing from the corner of his mouth. He was reminded of the camel
earlier that day. Or was it a dromedary? Or was it yesterday? This
man was dangerous. He also seemed to have got the wrong end of
the stick and if his wife's insinuations at lunch were correct then
that was likely to prove bad news for Bognor.

"There seems to be some misunderstanding," said Bognor in
his politest voice.

"Too damn right, sonny," agreed Baker. He sloshed more
Chivas into the glass and relit the cigar which had gone out,
neglected during his bout of ill temper.

"What have you done with her?"

"What do you mean? *Who?*" Bognor decided to act dumb.

"Jesus! You bum! I suppose you were at some damn fancy English version of Upper Canada College. You got her set up in some
apartment someplace. Who *are* you anyway?"

"Bognor. Board of Trade."

"Bognor. Board of Trade," mimicked Baker, pseudo English accent thick with alcohol and a rotten imitation in any case. "What
in hell does that mean? That's a place, not a person."

"With respect," said Bognor, still longing for a glass of water
but thinking it unwise to repeat the request, "if you would only
stop to listen I am trying to tell you that you are barking up the
wrong tree. I hardly know your wife. I don't even particularly
fancy her."

"You what!?" Baker half rose from his chair and then subsided.
He was angrier than ever. "Are you telling me you don't fancy my
wife? Goddamn, you first commit adultery with my wife and
then, so help me, you tell me you don't fancy her. I will kill you
with my bare hands if it's the last thing I do, so help me."

The phone on his desk rang and he scooped up the receiver in
a trembling hand while the other refilled the glass. Bognor
reckoned Baker would pass out before long. A quarter of the bottle had gone down his gullet already and they had hardly started.

"Where in hell are you?" Baker shouted into the telephone. "I
know where you are, you're at this guy's apartment. Yeah, Bognor. I'm coming right down there soon as I've dealt with him.
Sure, he's right here. . . . No, you cannot. Are you joking? You
have to be joking. . . . Honey, give me just one good reason why

I should believe one lying word you say to me. . . . Because you are trying to ruin me, that's for why. . . . You better get yourself one good lawyer, hon, because that's what you're gonna need. . . . What I do with him is my affair. . . . You do that. You just do that. You just go right ahead and you do just that thing. . . . Hello . . . Hello." And he crashed the receiver onto its cradle.

"Tell me"—Bognor felt suddenly lightheaded—"did you kill Farquhar?" It seemed the obvious question. The man was about to kill him, or have him killed by his gorillas, for cuckolding him. The fact that Bognor was innocent of this was neither here nor there. If Baker was going to kill now for love, or for damaged *amour-propre*—or whatever it was that he imagined had been done to him—then he could have killed first time round.

He did not appear to have heard the question for he was sitting at the desk staring blankly at the phone.

"Let me put it another way." tried Bognor. "Did you get a present of rather special Balenciaga bath oil last Christmas?"

Still Baker said nothing. Then, just as Bognor was about to rephrase the question for the third time, the cuckolded tycoon looked up at him with an expression of manic malevolence. It was an expression which haunted Bognor for the rest of his life but he did not have long to absorb it, for an instant later Baker picked up the first thing that came to hand and threw it hard straight at his prisoner, striking him above the temple. Bognor managed to duck his head in time to avoid being hit in the eyes, which was just as well for a smashing bottle of Chivas Regal could well have blinded him. As it was he simply passed out.

This time he came round under more pleasant circumstances. He woke to find himself in bed. The room appeared to be decorated entirely in different shades of white. Even the solicitous people dimly observed through the one eye which he apprehensively opened and then shut at once seemed to be more than usually white. It hurt to open the eye so he kept it closed. He was pleased to hear a soothing female voice seconds later and to feel a cool damp cloth being applied to his brow with gentle ministering hands. He listened briefly to kind, efficient voices, one male, one female, conferring in muted tones. Thus comforted, he returned to sleep.

Some time later he came round again and opened both eyes to be rewarded with the sight of Louise Poitou gazing down at him with an expression of apparently anguished concern. He was unable to focus very well but she seemed ever more attractive than usual when observed in this soft blurred way. He tried smiling but found it hurt so returned his mouth to a position of repose. Then he made an effort to speak but ceased before he began because that too caused pain.

"Don't say anything," said Louise. "You're going to be all right."

It had not occurred to Bognor that he was *not* going to be all right, so that this well-intentioned sentence did not have quite the desired effect. He tried to sit up, but immediately experienced severe shooting pains all over his body.

"Don't move," whispered Louise putting a restraining hand on his shoulder. "There's rather a lot broken."

"Like what?" he asked hoarsely, even those two words costing more than they were worth.

"Oh, a couple of ribs, and a leg. Otherwise it's just heavy bruising. And concussion. They were worried about a skull fracture and brain damage at first, but your skull's intact and the brain is fine."

Bognor was relieved to hear it.

"They found you on the Don Valley Parkway," she continued, "under one of the bridges, the favourite suicide spot. That's what they thought at first. That you were a failed suicide, the first ever you'd have been, because that bridge is so high no one makes mistakes. Then when they smelt the booze and saw the blood they decided you were a traffic case. Hit and run. It wasn't till they got you in here and found the marks on your wrists and ankles that they started to treat it as an attempted murder. Then your friend Smith of the RCMP showed up and he's dealing with it. He's going to try to get a statement as soon as you're fit."

"How . . ." Bognor began, but the effort cost him too much and he stopped.

"Don't ask questions," she said. "I'll just try to give you the answers. I got in because I said I was your girlfriend. I hope you don't mind." She faltered. "Oh, Simon," she said, "I'm so sorry. It was my fault. It was crazy to do it, but it never occurred to me that the guy was so paranoid. He had thugs following Maggie wherever she went. Just to catch her out with a man. They thought it was an assignation."

She paused, sounding quite overcome.

"They may not let me have very long, Simon. You're not supposed to be tired. There are just two points you have to remember, when Smith comes for your statement. The first is that he is convinced, but convinced, that you were roughed up by the Quebecois. By Seven, in fact. Jean-Claude is in the clear. He can prove where he was all that day and nothing Smith can do will break that alibi. The other thing is that Johnny Baker is very big in this town. No one will believe you if you try to blame him for what happened. It will do you no good even to suggest it. It is much better not even to mention it."

Bognor nodded. Out of the corner of his better eye he was aware that another person had come into his room. A woman in white.

"Nurse wants me to go now," said Louise softly. "Maggie sends her love. She is safe and in the country. Remember what I say. I will come again soon, meanwhile take care, eh?"

And she leaned over and kissed him gently on each cheek.

Bognor managed an agonizing half smile. He had always found deathbed scenes romantic and this, though more painful than he would have wished, showed signs of having moments to recommend it. He closed his eyes and slipped back into merciful sleep.

When he woke next the pain was worse and he felt a great deal more alert. On the whole he preferred a more painless, drug-dulled state, but he supposed he was going to have to become used to the sordid business of living again. The nurse was bending over him. This time she was in sharp focus.

"Your friend Pete Smith is here," she said. "Do you feel well enough to see him?"

"No," said Bognor, "but I will. Show him in."

He had not the slightest wish to see Smith. He knew all too well how he would behave and he was not mistaken.

"Hi, Simon. How ya doin?" the Mountie asked boisterously. In his hands he held a bunch of black grapes and a green creeping thing in a pot. "Gee, they sure gave you a hard time," he said, giving Bognor a genial once-over. "Would you recognize any of them?"

"Not sure," said Simon. "Doubt it."

Smith put the plant on the bedside table and helped himself to a handful of grapes.

"Wanna talk about it?"

"Not particularly, but I will if you want me to."

"I'd appreciate it." He took out a notebook and a ballpoint pen. "Okay," he said. "Shoot."

"Where do you want me to start?"

"At the beginning, I guess, Simon."

"I'm not sure where that is."

The Mountie shifted his gum from one cheek to the other and laughed explosively.

"Glad to see you've kept your sense of humour," he said. "So what happened?"

"Someone hit me on the head."

"Any idea who?"

"None whatever. He hit me from behind."

"Where was this?"

"At the zoo."

"The zoo?" Smith gave Bognor a hard look. "You keen on animals?"

"Not particularly. I went skiing."

Another hard, sceptical look. "You keen on skiing?"

"Not particularly. That is to say, I, er, well, let's just say I thought I'd give it a whirl."

"A whirl?"

"A whirl. A try. I thought I'd try it. To see what it was like." God, thought Bognor, the man is an imbecile.

"So you were out skiing at the zoo and this French bastard comes up behind you and thumps you?"

"I don't know he was French. Otherwise yes."

"Any witnesses?"

"No. Except there was more than one of them. Three, in fact."

"*Three* French bastards?"

"If you insist."

Smith wrote eagerly, flicking his chewing gum about as he did. "So you're in the zoo, skiing all on your own and suddenly you're jumped by these three French bastards. Then what?"

"I woke up in the boot of this car."

"In the boot! Holy mackerel!"

"What do you mean?"

"What sort of car was this, Si? I mean you should have fried to death stuck in there in the engine. I don't see how they found room for you in there."

"In the boot, not under the bonnet." Simon hurt and he was exasperated. "I don't know what sort of car it was. I was in the back and the engine was up front."

"Oh," said Smith. "So you were in the trunk, not the boot."

"For God's sake," said Bognor. "I was in the part of the car where you put suitcases. Now can we get on? I'm not well."

"Okay, steady on, Simon." Smith wrote ponderously. "I know how you feel but I have a job to do and I intend nailing these French bastards if it's the last thing I do."

Bognor closed his eyes and prayed for patience.

"Then what?" asked Smith.

"Then I was taken out of the car and they hit me about a bit more and I must have passed out because I woke up here."

"Where was this?"

"A big house. A bit like Harrison Bentley's in Rosedale."

"Are you telling me you were beaten up at Harrison Bentley's house?"

"No, in a house *like* Harrison Bentley's."

And so the questioning ground on. Bognor managed to avoid saying anything about Johnny Baker or his wife or Louise. He also managed to avoid anything as potentially dangerous as a direct lie. Finally Smith was told by the sympathetic nurse that he was tiring the patient and that he must rest. No sooner had Smith been ejected, having eaten all but a handful of his grapes, than Louise was shown in.

CHAPTER 8

Bognor was becoming quite used to having her around now and although it could scarcely be said that they enjoyed anything even approaching a relationship he was beginning to believe in their little subterfuge.

"Hello, girlfriend," he croaked, voice exhausted from answering Smith's tiresome questions, "what's the news from the great outdoors?"

She pulled a face. "Not so good. Jean-Claude was taken in for questioning. Three hours they kept him. He said they were very polite. That is always a bad sign."

"And you. Have they questioned you?"

"Not so much. They don't know I am a friend of Maggie's. And they don't know I am seeing you." She smiled. She was in jeans and a crisp white shirt today. Very neat and trim. "You didn't tell your friend that you were at the zoo with Maggie and me, did you?"

"He's not my friend. And no. Have a grape. I don't care for them. Present from the Mounties."

"No, thank you. How are you feeling?"

"I thought you'd never ask. So-so. Better, I think. But they're not giving me so much painkiller so it *feels* worse, if you follow." He lay back and wallowed. It was good to be fussed over. He was inclined to agree with what she had said the other night on the island. It didn't really matter who killed Farquhar. The world was well shot of him. He was not much missed. He smiled. She smiled. "Are you still going to have dinner with me?"

"Of course. There's just one condition."

"You mean . . ." His voice trailed away. Outside in the corridor he heard voices raised in argument. One voice was persistent, authoritative, cool, Canadian, the other was persistent, authoritative, shrill, English. They were getting nearer.

"Oh," said Bognor, gulping hard. "I'm afraid our dinner is suddenly at risk. I'm afraid that's the first Mrs. Bognor you hear without."

Louise gave him a shy grin of delicious complicity, which was to haunt him for years. "I'd better go," she said.

"Um," said Bognor, not wishing to seem ungallant, but feeling apprehensive. "You might be well advised."

"There's only one way out," she giggled. "It's like Feydeau."

"That's exactly what it's *not* like," he said. "In Feydeau there are always other ways out. Lots of them. That's the whole point of Feydeau."

The door opened. The nurse was doing her best to play immoveable object but to no avail. She had her back to the door but she was being pushed, quite literally, through it. Monica was taller than her and could see over the nurse's shoulder and into the room as soon as the door gave way.

"Simon. Darling. You look ghastly," she said.

Bognor smiled as brightly as possible. "Not too hot, actually."

"I came as soon as I heard. I only got in an hour ago, I came straight from the airport." She took in Louise for the first time, registered slight shock followed by disapproval and marginal alarm all in quick succession before breeding got the better of her.

"Hello," she said, putting out her hand. "I don't think we've met. I'm Monica Bognor."

"Louise Poitou."

They shook hands. Bognor looked on grimly.

"I was just leaving, Mrs. Bognor. I only came by for a moment. I have an appointment at the university."

"Oh, don't go on my account," said Monica, beaming.

"No really, I must rush." Louise, halfway to the door, made a play of looking at her watch and letting out a little gasp of incredulity and Gallic horror. "Good-bye, Simon. Good-bye, Mrs. Bognor," she said, breathlessly, "I'll see you soon." And she was gone.

"Nice girl," said Monica, sitting down and delivering a somewhat perfunctory peck on the Bognor forehead. "Pretty too. French?"

"Well, you know, Quebecois. As a matter of fact she's a girlfriend of the main suspect. That's how I met her."

"How interesting," she said. "Darling, I mean it. You do look perfectly frightful. Even worse than I expected. I've been desperately worried. You are an incredible BF. Parkinson is livid with rage."

Dear old Monica, thought Bognor. A good sort. He was glad he'd married her. No doubt about it. He was fond of the old thing. And she wasn't bad-looking. In her own particular sort of way, and even if she wasn't to everyone's taste she was no slouch when it came to—well, no one could accuse *her* of not being about to function properly. Not that there would be much question of that with two broken ribs and a leg in plaster. Still, they would have to cross that bridge when they came to it.

"Parkinson has no business being livid with rage," he said. "If anyone has a right to be livid with rage then it's me."

"He thinks you're an idiot," said Monica. "I mean deep down underneath it all he's really quite fond of you but he thinks you're an idiot. And one has to admit that he does have a point."

"Thanks for the sympathy."

"Don't be silly." She plucked a grape. "You know perfectly well I'm sympathetic. I'm also a realist where you're concerned and it's my opinion that you're not safe to be allowed out on your own."

"The only reason," said Bognor, stuffily, "that I got hit on the head and beaten up is that I'm onto something."

"Oh, darling, you *always* say that. Nice grapes." She walked over to the window. "Did that little French girl bring them?"

"No, as a matter of fact it was that oaf from the Mounties. Smith."

"I spoke to him on the phone. He was the one who told me what had happened. He sounded rather nice as a matter-of-fact. Sensible too. He seemed to think it was something to do with the French."

"He's an imbecile," said Bognor. "He thinks everything is to do with the French."

"Well then if it isn't to do with the French what is it to do with?"

"Sex," said Bognor.

She spun round and regarded him superciliously. "Sometimes I think you're the imbecile. You think everything is to do with sex unless it's to do with food and drink."

"That's not even remotely fair," expostulated the patient, so far enjoying the conjugal cut and thrust that he was beginning to forget how much he hurt.

"In this particular case, as it happens, the late Sir Roderick Farquhar, a nasty piece of work with a keen eye for the ladies, had enticed away the wife of a rival tycoon, an equally nasty piece of work named Johnny Baker. When Mrs. Baker tried to drop Farquhar he didn't like it so he sent all her love letters to Baker. Baker is impotent. So he killed Farquhar."

Monica elevated her eyebrows in an expression of intense scepticism. "I don't think much of that as a theory," she said mildly. "Where did you find it?"

"The girl told me."

"What girl?"

"The one who was married to Baker. *Is* married to Baker. She told me at the zoo."

"Another girl," observed Monica acidly.

"She's a friend of Louise's. I was at the zoo with both of them."

"I see." Monica sounded long-suffering. She had been here too often before to take much pleasure in it. "So this girl told you that her husband killed Farquhar?"

"More or less."

"Odd thing to tell you." Monica took another grape. "Wouldn't you say? Even if your husband is impotent."

"Then I was jumped by these three gorillas, figuratively speaking, that is."

"And the girls?"

"They got away."

Monica's eyebrows threatened to disappear altogether. "Convenient," she said. "And I suppose now you're going to tell me you were taken to this other tycoon's house and beaten up for having it off with his wife at the zoo."

"Yes. In fact that's almost exactly what happened. Apart from anything else he threw a bottle of Chivas Regal at me when I accused him of killing Farquhar."

"Oh, Simon!" She appeared to choke on a grape. "You must admit, it's quite funny."

"Hilarious," said Bognor dryly. "They suspected brain damage. *And* a skull fracture."

"No, not that," she grinned. "I really am very sympathetic about that. It's the idea of your making off with this tycoon's wife at the zoo. Was she sexy?"

"Yes," said Bognor. "Very."

"Oooh," said Monica. "Temper!"

"No, really, Monica." Bognor assumed his stroppiest voice. "It's all very well. I do my best for queen and country and all you do is mock."

"I'm not mocking, Simon. Really. Mind if I finish the grapes?" She picked the last one without waiting for an answer. "It's been a rotten experience and I've been very worried. And now I'm going to nurse you through a gentle convalescence and we can forget all about the whole absurd business."

"It's still got to be solved."

"But not by you, dear."

"I'm still on the case," he remonstrated. "Just because of all this doesn't mean to say I'm giving up. Not just when I'm getting somewhere. And I've had no instructions from Parkinson."

"Parkinson gave me firm instructions to make sure you lie doggo. I'm to supervise your recovery and then bring you home."

"But meanwhile I'm still investigating the Farquhar murder."

"Nominally. You'll have to check with Parkinson."

"He can't object if I just talk to one or two people."

Monica looked doubtful. "The trouble with your talks is that they always seem to lead to such fearful arguments," she said. "Who do you want to talk to?"

"All the people that Farquhar gave bath oil to for Christmas."

Monica sighed deeply, then sat down on the bed, causing his

broken leg to swing slightly from the pulley which was holding it up at a forty-five-degree angle.

"God! Careful!" he shouted.

She got up quickly.

"We'll see," said Monica, "and now I must be going. I'm using your hotel room, which, obviously you won't be needing for a while. Parkinson said the Board will pay."

After she had gone, the nurse came in, looking mischievous and conspiratorial. She held an envelope.

"Oh, dear, Mr. Bognor," she said, her Canadian accent, he realized for the first time, heavily overlaid with Scottish, "we've been a naughty boy." She favoured him with a schoolmistressy expression which mixed censure with amusement in equal quantities. "Your friend asked me to give you this. She quite forgot, in the confusion."

He did not read it until she had changed his dressings and tidied his bed. When he opened it he found that it was not from Louise but Jean-Claude. It was a list of Farquhar's Christmas gifts from last year. Just enough of his friends and acquaintances had received bath oil to make it intriguing.

He mended rapidly and he was a bad patient. His injuries turned out to be less severe—though no less painful—than originally supposed: more cracks than breaks. This meant that he earned an early discharge and was able to leave hospital at the end of a week. He spent his time in bed trying to read the novels of Robertson Davies and Margaret Laurence, making lists and thinking.

The lists were virtually identical and went as follows:

SUSPECTS ON THE SPOT: Jean-Claude Prideaux. Opportunity: innumerable. Motive, political?

Amos Littlejohn. Opportunity: as above. Motive: to benefit from will (not very strong but must talk).

SUSPECTS NOT ON SPOT BUT WITH MURDER WEAPONS AT HAND (viz. bottles of bath oil):

Mr. and Mrs. Ainsley Cernik

Dolores V. Crump (alias *La Bandanna Rouge*)

Colonel Crombie (Senior Vice-President Mammoncorp)

The Honourable John C. Baker (The bath oil had, somewhat indiscreetly, been given to Maggie.)

Harrison Bentley

Opportunities: All had bottles of oil. These could have been opened, diluted with crystals of phosphorus trioxide, resealed and insinuated into Farquhar's own personal supply. N.B. Could it? If Farquhar had many boxes of oil what guarantee was there that oil would be used this year, next year, sometime, never? Presumably Littlejohn kept a small supply with him to put in place when the old bottles ran out.

At this point the scribblings disintegrated and went off on any number of different tangents until in exasperation he crumpled them into balls and threw them at the wastepaper basket, usually missing. Twice a day Monica called, bringing with her a brace of peach-blossom yoghurt shakes from the stall in the rabbit warren below the Sheraton Hotel. She would pick up the balls of paper, occasionally trying to decipher them. Then she would ask, "Penny for your thoughts?"

He was not always able to reply honestly to this because he found himself frequently thinking about Louise. She, presumably discomfitted by her encounter with the first Mrs. Bognor, had made no effort to resume contact. Despite his efforts to dismiss her he found that the more she was out of sight, the more she was in his mind. His other dominant thought was that he must visit Amos Littlejohn as soon as possible. When he mentioned this to Monica she merely smiled and said that they would have to see.

After three days he had a phone call from Parkinson.

"Your wife tells me you're on the mend," he said breezily.

"Ah."

"Once you're out of that place you're to take a month's leave."

"But—"

"No buts. I want you fit and well and raring to go."

"What about the Farquhar case?"

"I've spoken to all the necessary people and we can regard that as settled. I'm told there'll be an arrest as soon as the political situation allows."

"You mean Prideaux."

"Correct."

"But I don't think he did it."

"What's the weather like out there?"

"Where I am it's about eighty degrees Fahrenheit twenty-four hours round the clock," said Bognor. "I want to talk to someone called Amos Littlejohn."

"With what object in view?" Parkinson sounded abstracted.

"He was Farquhar's manservant."

"I told you the case is closed. I don't want you being beaten up again. And I don't want any unpleasantness with the Canadians."

"If I'm on leave I can do what I like."

"Bognor"—Parkinson's voice sounded bored and irritated—"I don't frankly give a damn what you do with your leave provided you report back here in a fit state when it's over. The only other stipulation I make is that you keep that wife of yours by your side at all times. At all times. She is all that stands between you, me and an institute for the criminally insane."

"Thanks very much," said Bognor. "See you anon."

Which explains how, in part, a week later Bognor and Monica were driving north to the Farquhar stud. Littlejohn, who had served Farquhar faithfully for years, had inherited his horses. This was a sufficiently generous bequest to rank as a motive since the Farquhar horses were world-famous—genuinely so. Even those whose interest in horses extended only to an annual flutter on the Kentucky or Epsom Derbies had heard of such Farquhar thoroughbreds as Byron, Fraser Canyon and Richibucto. Both of the last two now stood at stud on the Farquhar ranch by the shores of Lake Simcoe just south of Barrie. They would make Littlejohn rich.

"I still think this is silly," said Monica for the tenth time that morning. Bognor sat in the passenger seat of the cumbersome hired Ford, his crutches stowed in the back. "Shouldn't we have said we were coming?"

"He'd have refused to see us."

"Quite right. Then we couldn't have gone."

"Oh, Monica," said Bognor, "I love you dearly, but I do wish you'd see my point of view."

"It's not a point of view," she replied with asperity. "It's a feeling in your bones. Or"—she stabbed at the accelerator pedal—"more likely in your gut. What are you going to say when we get there?"

"That we just happened to be passing by."

"On our way from Toronto to the Arctic Circle. Just a little routine jaunt. Ha bloody ha! Do be your age. You don't expect him to believe it, do you?"

"No, but one has to say something. It's merely a convention."

The snow had melted several days ago and the world was dull grey as they turned off the highway and took the lanes to Farquhar Farms Inc. The country was gently undulating, thinly populated, the only buildings being huge Ontario barns, neat wooden farmhouses and the occasional white clapboard church with a tiny tower and belfry. "This should be it," said Bognor as they came on newly painted white fencing enclosing fields of lawnlike grass. One or two shining horses grazed gently. In the field nearest them a stallion was charging at the rails, halting just short of them, pawing the ground then turning to gallop to the other end of the field, flicking its heels and tossing its head as it went. Half a mile farther on they came to a tarmac drive which led between an avenue of conifers to a large colonial mansion with high columns supporting a central arch. The Canadian flag dropped from a pole above the front door. Monica slowed the car to walking pace.

"Yes?" she enquired.

"Yes, please," he said.

"On your head then," and she turned and drove slowly over the "sleeping policemen," the tarmac bumps in the road designed to slow the reckless driver. Halfway along the drive Bognor called to her to stop for a second. On a short stretch of railway line stood a highly polished purple wagon-lit with a golden legend inscribed on its side: Spirit of Saskatoon.

"Touch morbid," said Bognor. "He met his end in that thing."

"Not still in there, is he?" asked his wife, regarding the sleeping car dubiously.

"What, stuffed, I suppose?"

"Well. It would make an imposing mausoleum," she said. "Not quite Castle Howard but with a touch of the requisite eccentricity."

"Okay." Bognor nodded towards the house. "Let's see if His Nibs is in. We can always ask for a guided tour. I must say, I wasn't expecting it here."

They parked by the front door, which opened as they stopped to reveal a butler in short black coat, striped trousers and a grey silk tie. He appeared to be the genuine article since he spoke in the scrupulously well modulated tones of the upper echelons of the servants' hall. He wanted, he said, to know if he could be of any assistance. Bognor, still not used to his crutches, hovered uncertainly in the driveway while Monica fished a visiting card from her husband's inside breast pocket.

The butler took it, examined it with a butler's patronizing air, and disappeared to see if his newly elevated master was at home. A few minutes later he reemerged to say that Mr. Littlejohn would see them now. They were ushered in, Bognor swinging along like Long John Silver, and taken along a high passage lined with family portraits of doubtful authenticity until they arrived in a conservatory where a fat black man in blue canvas shorts, a Harvard University T-shirt and sneakers lay in a hammock eating a banana. As they entered he rolled out of the hammock and walked towards them, tossing the banana skin in the direction of a potted palm.

"Mr. Bognor," he said, extending a welcoming hand. "What a pleasant surprise. You were involved in the Gentleman's Relish Affair, I recall. We never met. But Sir Roderick spoke most warmly of you."

"Oh, God," thought Bognor, "a character."

"I just happened to be passing by," he said, out loud, "and I thought I'd take the liberty of dropping in. Allow me to introduce my wife, Monica."

Mr. Littlejohn beamed and said he was charmed. He offered them a drink. The butler was sent off for champagne, an old habit of Sir Roderick's and one which Mr. Littlejohn was keeping on.

"I'm sorry to see you've been in the wars, Mr. Bognor," he said, indicating the crutches and Bognor's plastered foot.

"Skiing accident," said Bognor.

"So you are here on holiday?"

"Yes."

"Aha." Mr. Littlejohn pressed pink palms together and contemplated them. "A pity. I had thought for a moment that this might be a business visit. I would have enjoyed the opportunity of discussing my late master's unhappy death."

"Well," Bognor was slightly nonplussed by this. He had dreamed up a long, convoluted conversational gambit which would have led to the raising of the subject of the murder in about twenty minutes' time. This was not what he had expected. "Um, just because I'm off duty doesn't mean to say I can't . . . Well, as it happens there are one or two loose ends that have been puzzling me."

Mr. Littlejohn demurred. "I would not think of intruding on your holiday by raising matters of professional interest. Besides, the whole question is still sub judice and it would therefore be improper of us to as much as mention it. Is my interpretation of the law correct?"

"There's the letter of the law and the spirit of the law," said Bognor, tentatively. "Not always the same thing."

Monica gave him a daggerish look.

"You could say," he continued, "that although I'm not officially dealing with the case, my presence in Canada is not entirely coincidental."

Mr. Littlejohn rubbed his hands and beamed. "Aha," he said again, "I understand perfectly. You can rely on my total discretion. Mum is the word, eh." And he laughed immoderately and invited them to lunch, an invitation which Bognor accepted with alacrity although Monica, making a mouth like a prune, was obviously going to have fierce words to say later.

It would be wrong to describe Mr. Littlejohn as a perfect witness since his orotund manner of speaking meant that it took him longer than most people to say what he wanted. His use of vocabulary was uncertain and tended towards malapropism so that Bognor was not always entirely sure that he understood exactly what he was telling him. But the gist was plain enough.

First of all it seemed that the deceased was not a well man. Every morning and every evening Littlejohn had put out piles of pills for his master to consume. Liver pills, heart pills, vitamins, pills for lowering and raising blood pressure—Mr. Littlejohn had little or no idea what the pills were supposed to do. Without them, however, Sir Roderick was convinced that he was a goner. Nor was this just hypochondria. At least twice within the last five years he had been to hospital to have bits removed. Mr. Littlejohn thought a lung had gone in one visit and a piece of intestine in the other. He was unable to be more precise. Sir Roderick's doctor was in Harley Street. He had a Canadian doctor, a quite competent physician, but not trusted. Sir Roderick's advice to Littlejohn had been much the same as that given on behalf of Sir Winston Churchill in relation to *his* doctor, Lord Moran.

"If Sir Winston is taken ill, call Lord Moran and get him to send for a doctor." Littlejohn was happy to furnish Bognor with the English doctor's name.

Secondly Littlejohn could not explain how or when the lethal bath oil was substituted for the innocent bottle. The bath oil was kept in crates of twenty bottles in Farquhar's personal stores. Whenever necessary Littlejohn got out a new case. This accompanied him wherever he went, though it was not guarded. Anyone knowing about it could have worked a switch if they could have got into the railway car, the private plane, any one of Sir Roderick's apartments or houses or offices. Littlejohn was also adamant that the only person who ever broke the seal of a bottle was Farquhar himself. A broken-sealed bottle would have to be put into Farquhar's medicine cabinet, not Littlejohn's crate, a much more difficult procedure since the only people who might have gone near it were personal staff, which meant, in practice, Littlejohn and Prideaux. He affected not to know that Sir Roderick had dished out bottles of the exclusive liquid as Christmas presents. Hitherto he had supposed that the murderer was Prideaux because he said only Prideaux would have had the necessary access. Also he did not trust him.

"Ah never did care for Frenchies," he said, "and in my esteem Mr. Prideaux was not a gennelman."

Finally, although he himself claimed absolute loyalty to his late employer, he confessed that he could be difficult. Sir Roderick, he agreed, had possessed more enemies than friends. Indeed it would be stretching a point to say that he had any friends at all.

"What about Mrs. Baker?" asked Bognor. "Wasn't she a friend?"

"No, sir," replied Mr. Littlejohn, tipsy on champagne of which he had produced a second bottle. "Mrs. Baker was a *girl*friend." He winked prodigiously. "Saving your presence, Mrs. Bognor, my former master and benefactor was some swordsman. I remember days when we was smuggling girls out the back door almost as soon as they came in the front. Don't ask me how he did it. Even when he was ill and old, he just could not get enough."

"Didn't anyone refuse him?" asked Monica.

"Not so's I remember, ma'am," said Littlejohn. "Course he wasn't always too choosy about who he had. And he had the money to make it worth their while."

"I gather Mrs. Baker refused to marry him." This from Bognor.

"He was mad as hell at her for something she did but I never did figure out what it was. Not my place to ask either."

"I understood it was because she wouldn't give up Mr. Baker and marry him instead."

"Sir Roderick he wanted just everything. His mouth was bigger than his stomach." Mr. Littlejohn scratched an ear thoughtfully. "And he just hated that Baker boy. He just hated him."

"Then why did he send him bath oil at Christmas? Some kind of a joke?"

"That I just wouldn't know."

"And did *he* send Baker all Mrs. Baker's love letters?" Littlejohn frowned. "That what you heard?" he asked.

"Yes," said Bognor.

"Well, if that's what you heard, then that's what you heard." He laughed. "For a gentleman who just happened to be passing by my vestibule you sure have an awful lot of questions to ask."

Bognor smiled nervously, Monica kicked him under the table,

and they spent the rest of the meal discussing Blenheim Palace, where, years before, Littlejohn had started life as a very junior footman. He told an outrageous story concerning the Prince of Wales.

Afterwards, the men both smoking six-inch Davidoffs (another little legacy of Sir Roderick's), they went outside to look at the horses and the Spirit of Saskatoon. This last had been preserved inside as well as out. The plovers' eggs, the Oxford marmalade and the notorious Gentleman's Relish were still in the galley. The ticker tape still held the last message Sir Roderick would ever have read, timed the night of his death, the closing price on the Tokyo Stock Exchange. In the wardrobe there were still half a dozen of Farquhar's suits and a brace of his distinctive canary-yellow waistcoats. In the bathroom the eighteenth-century Florentine tub in which the head of Mammoncorp had breathed his last, remained elegant as ever, a bottle of the murderous bath oil resting alongside the loofah on the soap tray alongside the walnut reading tray.

CHAPTER 9

"I didn't care for the Spirit of Saskatoon much," said Bognor, exhausted by the day. He had found smoking on crutches a considerable imposition.

"Like something from Madame Tussaud's," agreed Monica. "I'm not clear why he does it. He's not quite real either. Spooky."

"Worthwhile though."

"You think so?"

"I'm certainly going to have a word with that Harley Street quack."

"That's not going to help much. We know he didn't die of natural causes."

"Supposing he did though?" Bognor rubbed his chin.

"But he didn't."

"No."

Even so the idea haunted him.

That evening they had dined at the Courtyard, where Toronto's trendies gathered at lunch to drink Perrier water. Bognor had enjoyed it on his earlier visit to the city. It was one of the few places where he didn't find the profusion of indoor greenery unduly botanical. And the food was straightforward.

"It's almost as if the old buzzard was setting everyone up," he said. "He sends out murder weapons to a whole gang of people, most of whom apparently hate him, and he as good as says, 'Go ahead shoot me.'" He stuffed his mouth full of spinach and bacon salad, and sipped Inniskillin. "This is the only decent wine in the whole of Ontario," he said. "It's really not bad. Not for the likes of Farquhar though."

They both finished their first course in silence, then inspected the room for further topics of conversation. It had that peculiarly

Toronto quality of first-generation chic which Bognor found
rather charming and Monica found rather absurd. They both felt
as if the entire city and its inhabitants had been designed by a
firm of interior designers in the late sixties and early seventies.

"It's so self-conscious," opined Monica, gazing critically at a
leggy Negress in cavalry twill trousers and a tweed hacking jacket
who was talking to an intense balding man in a white suit and
tinted spectacles. "Is this one of Farquhar's haunts?"

"No. There's a place called Winston's which is about the only
restaurant he was ever seen in. Instant stuffiness. Ties and jackets
and a hint of yesterday's cigar smoke," said Bognor. "They spray
it on, I'm sure. Baker goes there too. I don't think what they call
'old money' dines out in restaurants. They prefer each other's
houses."

"What about that lot then?" asked Monica, swivelling her eyes
in the direction of a chef who was slicing mushrooms like a
human Magimix. "No, not there, stupid. Just behind the oasis.
By the fig trees and the pampas grass. The woman in the emerald
feathers. That has to be old money, surely."

Bognor turned awkwardly. His injuries made neck movement
uncomfortable so that he had to turn his trunk as well. Since that
was also uncomfortable he spent most of his time staring straight
ahead.

"God, yes!" he exclaimed, turning back with injudicious alacrity and pretending to be engrossed in the entrecote with poivres
verts which had just been put in front of him. "That's Harrison
Bentley and his wife Muriel. And friends. Don't know who the
feathers belong to. Or who the chap is. Same sort of people by
the look of it." He grinned. "Nouveau old money if you follow
me. Total phoney."

"And another murder suspect?" Monica was having some sort
of chicken with cream and brandy and truffles. She was accompa-
nying it with a gratin dauphinoise. Bognor reflected that if she
went on like this she was going to get fat. Not that he could talk.
On the other hand it was different for a man and in any case he
wasn't able to take exercise at the moment. If he could have gone
skiing every day his paunch would be more manageable.

"He had bath oil," agreed Bognor, "and he obviously disliked

Farquhar. If he did him in it would have been for quasi-business reasons." He cut into his steak, another manoeuvre made painful by injury. "One thing about Canada," he said. "They certainly know how to make steak."

"Do people murder each other for business reasons?" asked Monica. "I thought the stab in the back in the boardroom was just a figure of speech."

"It's possible," said Bognor. "Bentley is so snobbish and besotted with 'the mother country' that he could have done it. I suspect what really rankled was Farquhar's knighthood. Parkinson won't like it though. I'm supposed to make sure that Bentley and his cronies win out in the boardroom battle against the Cerniks. That will be a victory for Britain."

"Don't look now," said Monica, "but I think they're coming over."

Bognor, whose immediate reaction to "don't look now" was to look at once, began to turn but decided he had experienced enough pain for one meal and took another stab at the beef. He had just got a forkful into his mouth when he heard the unmistakeably laundered Old Money, Rosedale, Mother Country voice of Mr. Bentley. Canglish, thought Bognor, that's what it was, not a real language at all but an invention like Esperanto or Franglais.

"Good evening to you, Mr. Bognor," intoned Bentley, the greeting seeming to emanate from his nostrils.

"Oh," said Bognor. "Ah." He swallowed hard, not having chewed for the requisite twenty-five chews nannies insist on, grabbed for a glass of water, half rose in his chair, remembered his game leg, subsided, coughed, spluttered, was, in short, discomfitted.

"Please don't get up, Mr. Bognor. I'm exceedingly sorry to see that you've been in the wars."

"Skiing accident," said Bognor, clearing the blocked tubes. "Silly of me."

"You know my wife, Muriel, Mr. Bognor." Muriel, at her husband's elbow, simpered and said something unintelligible but affably intentioned.

"I don't think you know *my* wife, Monica, Mr. Bentley," entering into the courtly spirit of the proceedings. He was certainly not going to destroy Bentley's view of the English by being boorish. Monica smiled, inclined her head and held out a hand in a passable imitation of the Queen Mother at a Variety Club gala. Bognor was proud of her.

"Permit me to introduce Miss Dolores Crump," said Bentley, indicating the woman in the green feathers who had first attracted Monica's attention. Bognor made a token attempt to stand and Miss Crump acknowledged it with a mute gesture which said, "Please, not on my account," though Bognor gained the impression that she would have enjoyed seeing him inflict grievous bodily harm on himself in order to pay her proper respect. She looked hard as tin tacks, of a certain age, outrageously painted and feathered, and slim to the point of being bony. Like an ageing parakeet. So this was Farquhar's last mistress. Or last publicly acknowledged "live-in girlfriend." Her eyelids matched her feathers and since she appeared to spend a lot of time with her eyes closed one saw a lot of them. Bognor wondered if they shone in the dark. They *looked* luminous. As she moved across to exchange hand shakes with Monica (hers exaggeratedly limp, Monica's correspondingly beefy), a trim dapper gentleman, the fourth member of the party, said to Bognor,

"I'm Crombie, Mr. Bognor, pleased to meet you."

Bognor liked the look of him. A board member, prime suspect of course, but where Bentley, who this evening sported a red carnation in his buttonhole, seemed a papier-mâché figure, a forlorn imitation of a figment of his own imagination, Colonel Crombie appeared altogether more substantial. He was only little, small as a jockey, in fact, but although he must have been in his late sixties or early seventies he seemed fit and alert. His little eyes, rodent-black, flashed and crinkled at the corners in a way which suggested laughter, though Bognor couldn't see that he would get many laughs with the feathery Bandanna Rose.

Bognor decided to call him "sir." "Good evening, sir," he said.

"I've heard a great deal about you, Mr. Bognor." He sounded as if, for once, this might have been true. "Both from Muriel and Harrison here and from my old colleague Roddie Farquhar."

Bognor noticed that Colonel Crombie was careful not to claim anything as hypocritical as friendship with Sir Roderick. "There are one or two things I'd like to discuss with you. Would you lunch one day? Tomorrow perhaps. My club? The Royal Canadian Naval and Military, a thousand and one University. Corner of University and Dundas. Twelve forty-five? I look forward to it."

He shook hands with Monica, and the party withdrew.

"What was all that about?" she asked, mouth full of rich chicken and potato, neglected in these social niceties and growing cold.

"He wants a word," said Bognor, "about the murder, I should guess."

"Is he a suspect too?"

"Of course," he said. "La Bandanna too."

"The sooner," said Monica, "we get you safely home, the happier I shall be."

The Royal Canadian Naval and Military was modelled closely on its London counterparts around Pall Mall. Its hall was marble-floored and hung with green felt noticeboards announcing the election of new members, the death of old ones, cricket matches, increased bar charges and a warning about late payment of subscriptions. It boasted a brace of squash courts, a library with regimental magazines and other military publications, a bar, a card room and a dining room where the food was plain and plentiful. Its members tended towards moustaches and very short haircuts and the staff, apart from two buxom red-haired waitresses, were men grown old and faded in the service of their country. Their uniforms were old and faded too, so much so that as Bognor swung clumsily through the doors, obligingly held open for him by a hall porter in soup-stained livery with brass buttons dull with neglect, he felt quite at home. It scarcely mattered that the club was housed in the bottom two floors of a thirty-storey skyscraper. It was a convincing piece of lovingly manufactured reproduction and for Bognor the fact that it was an imitation enhanced rather than diminished it. He enjoyed the idea that someone had thought a London club worth imitating. There was no logic to this because he had despised Harrison Bentley's drawing room with its phoney efforts to ape upper-class England. Perhaps it was because he enjoyed nostalgia but despised snobbery. Or liked to think he did.

Colonel Crombie was waiting under an enormous oil painting of the British scaling the Heights of Abraham. It was a quite spectacularly dire bit of work, resembling, in this and other respects, those innumerable gory pictures found in military clubs and officers' messes throughout the world.

"I'm glad you could come, Mr. Bognor," said Crombie, detaching himself from a little group of moustachioed folk in tweeds and blazers. "Can I give you a hand with those crutches?"

"Thanks," said Bognor, stumbling slightly. "I'm afraid I haven't quite got the hang of them yet. There's a knack to it but I haven't mastered it."

"Haven't been on crutches since Dieppe," said Crombie. "Never figured them out until it was time to get rid of them and go back to managing on my own two legs." He laughed shortly and took Bognor by the elbow. "Luckily we have elevators here," he said. "In the old building you'd have had to deal with stairs but we're quite modern now. Come through and have a drink."

They moved clumsily into the bar, Bognor cursing his disability. It drew attention to himself, which he hated. He liked to merge with the wallpaper (which would have been difficult here since it was pea-green) and if there was one thing crutches did it was to interfere with one's natural anonymity. He accepted the colonel's offer of a dry martini and then regretted it when Crombie ordered himself a straight tomato juice with a liberal splashing of Worcester. The colonel did not, Bognor noted with approval, refer to the drink as a Virgin Mary.

"Don't mind my not drinking," he said, noticing Bognor's embarrassment. "I have meetings this afternoon and at my age I find I have to watch the alcohol intake. Used to be a bit of a boozer. Had to cut down, though. Come and sit down."

He led the way to a corner table with four low-backed leather chairs. Bognor fell into one and let his crutches fall to the floor with a clatter.

"Cheers," said Crombie, ignoring the fallen crutches, and wrinkling his nose over the tomato juice. "I hope you don't mind if we get down to brass tacks, straightaway. Never cared for that convention about not talking business till you've finished eating."

"Carry on," said Bognor, removing the olive from his drink and eating it.

"You're here to look into the Farquhar murder," said Crombie.

"In a manner of speaking." Bognor frowned. It was difficult to explain quite why he was here. He had virtually forgotten. Not that this was unusual. People had a habit of inviting him on assignations and then pretending to forget they had done so. This seemed to be the Mountie line of the moment.

"I was involved in the Gentleman's Relish business," he said.

Colonel Crombie nodded. "I remember only too well," he said. "You were wrong but for the right reasons."

"In a manner of speaking. I thought Sir Roderick was at the bottom of that but for once in his life he was innocent. All the same I knew he wasn't to be trusted."

Crombie chuckled. "You were right about that. A real corkscrew and yet you know I couldn't help being fond of him in a curious way."

"Oh." That had not been Bognor's problem. Nor anyone else's as far as he could ascertain. "We were sworn enemies, of course," Crombie continued, "which is why I could afford to like him. He was hell to his friends."

"I wouldn't have thought all his enemies were fond of him." Bognor thought of the Honourable John Baker.

"Oh, you needed a sense of humour to appreciate him," Colonel Crombie flicked a couple of peanuts into his mouth and smiled as if remembering some more than usually absurd incident. "He could be a funny, funny man. But as you have probably realized, a sense of humour is not the dominating Canadian characteristic."

"Leacock," ventured Bognor dubiously.

"Leacock was a Brit," said Crombie. "He just came to live here. Not half so funny as Farquhar in my view. The conceit of the man. Personalized Gentleman's Relish. Personalized Balenciaga bath oil. Personalized Krug. You couldn't take a man like that seriously, not if you had any feeling for the ridiculous. He was deeply absurd. I miss him a lot, if you must know."

"You're the first person who's said that."

"Really?" The colonel popped a couple more peanuts. "Well, that's a shame. But I'm sorry, I interrupted. You were telling me what exactly your role was in the investigation."

"Well," said Bognor. "When he was done in my people at the Board of Trade wanted me to come out and—this is between you and me—wanted me to come out and see that British interests didn't suffer unduly in the vacuum created, as it were, by Sir Roderick's death."

"I see." Colonel Crombie nodded. "Your guys don't want Mammoncorp pulling out of the sceptred isle. Correct?"

"Correct," said Bognor, "and the RCMP were prevailed upon to issue a formal invitation."

"I see." Crombie said this in a manner which suggested that he did not see much, nor clearly. "So," he said, in an effort to clarify the situation, "you're really here as an observer?"

"I don't have what you might call an executive responsibility," agreed Bognor, rather pleased with the phrase, "but the Mounties have told me, informally, that they have no objection to my pursuing my own independent enquiries."

"Hmmm." Crombie glanced at Bognor's glass, now almost empty. "Can I have that freshened up? Or would you rather go through and eat?" Bognor looked shiftily equivocal. He knew from experience that there would only be iced water with lunch. Colonel Crombie took the hint and snapped his fingers at a white-jacketed waiter.

"The RCMP officer in charge of the case seems to be someone named Pete Smith," said Colonel Crombie.

"Yes."

"Not a very live wire."

"Not very, no."

"My information"—Crombie spoke slowly, measuring the words—"is that he already has a good idea who was responsible."

"Yes, that's so."

"And do you agree with him?"

"I wouldn't go so far as to say that I disagree." Bognor disliked this sort of verbal fencing. "But the evidence is rather circumstantial. Or to be more precise, it's virtually nonexistent."

"Smith took a statement from me," said Crombie, "but he didn't seem very interested in getting any facts, more in confirming his prejudices."

Bognor said nothing.

"Do you agree?" asked his host.

Bognor smiled. "I wouldn't disagree," he said, for the second time.

The colonel seemed slightly discomfitted by this. Bognor, not wishing to seem discourteous or unhelpful, added, "My colleagues at the RCMP seem to think that the murder was politically motivated. They've established that the suspect—and I take it we're both talking about the same person—was a member of a secret association of Quebec partisans. Farquhar was passionately opposed to the Quebecois but, paradoxically, he wanted them to stay within the Dominion. Therefore he was murdered in order to prevent him using his power and influence to cripple Quebec. Q., as far as the Mounties are concerned, E.D."

"Farquhar was passionately opposed to Jews, blacks—always excepting old Amos—freemasons, homosexuals, and anyone who crossed him, including me. If it's motive you're looking for there's no problem. Most people who'd ever heard of him would have preferred him dead than alive."

"Including you?"

Crombie cocked his head on one side and looked at his half-empty glass quizzically. "Perfectly fair question," he said, "but first let me ask you one. Do you think I might have done it?"

"I think you *might* have done it," said Bognor, "which is not at all the same as thinking you did."

"Touché," laughed Crombie. "Okay. In answer to yours, no, I think I preferred having him alive. There were moments when I wished him dead. Many moments, but on the whole they passed off quite quickly. I'd say that I was happy for him to go on living. And I certainly couldn't have sustained a pathological ill will long enough for the premeditated killing. I might have slugged him at a board meeting but I'd never have gone to the trouble of fixing his bath oil." He paused and smiled, half mockingly at Bognor. "Do you buy that? Or do you think I'm lying?"

"I'll buy it for now," said Bognor.

"In that case let's go eat." Crombie got briskly to his feet and hauled Bognor laboriously to his. Bognor felt lightheaded from the martinis. He hoped he would be able to hang on to his crutches. On the other hand it was good to think that he had something to hang on to at moments like this. He wondered what Crombie was leading up to. Was it going to be merely a protestation of innocence—fairly superfluous in his case since he was not in Bognor's nor the Mounties' eyes a prime suspect.

"Let's not beat about the bush." They had ordered their meal and were waiting for soup. Crombie's manner was suddenly several degrees tougher. "My sources in Ottawa tell me there are going to be no arrests because of the political situation in Quebec."

Bognor said nothing at all and after a moment's silence Crombie continued, "I've talked to several members of the board and our view is that we can't afford to have this skeleton in our cupboard. We need a solution. And fast."

"I'm doing my best," said Bognor.

"Yeah. Well." Crombie paused while the optimistically designated potage bonne femme was set before them by one of the Irish waitresses. "As you've made clear, your part in these proceedings may not be central but it can be crucial. To be frank, Mr. Bognor, the lack of a solution is having an exceedingly adverse effect on company morale, and that is being reflected in the company's performance on the stock exchange. Do you read the city reports?"

Bognor had to confess that he did not.

"Well, as far as Mammon is concerned they're a real horror story right now."

"And that's because the Farquhar murder is still unsolved."

"That's my belief."

"Nothing to do with anything else. Your companies are sound and healthy in wind and limb?"

Crombie raised an eyebrow and broke his roll with a stabbing movement of finger and thumb. "You can take it from me, Mr. Bognor, that given the overall climate of recession there isn't a single division or subsidiary of Mammoncorp which isn't in terrific shape. Or wasn't until all this blew up."

"I don't see why solving the murder will improve your showing on the stock market."

"You'll just have to take that from me too."

"That's not good enough."

"No?" Crombie pushed aside his soup half finished. "I'm sorry," he said, "that soup is just terrible. I haven't had soup like that since I was stationed at Camberley. Listen, you may not realize it but this is a very small town, and in some ways it's a very small country. People talk. And right now people are talking their heads off about Mammoncorp. I hadn't realized just how bad it was, sitting down in my place in the Bahamas, not until I saw what was happening to the share prices. Then I hightailed it up here and I know at first hand."

"What exactly are they saying?" asked Bognor. "No one has said anything to me, and there's nothing in the papers."

"We don't have that kind of press," said Crombie, "and you're not talking to the right people. What they're saying is that there is a real scandal at Mammon and that the Farquhar murder is only the tip of the iceberg. They say that it's being hushed up in Ottawa, who have got a hold of the RCMP and won't let them make an arrest because of the scandal. They say that the murderer is going to get off because he's too damned powerful and he's being protected by government."

Their next course arrived. Steak and kidney pie. The vegetable claimed to be broccoli.

"Who are 'they'?" asked Bognor, spraying pepper over his food as if it were weed-killer.

" 'They' is everybody. Gossip. Informed talk. I don't know how you define it, but it exists in every community the world over. Since I've been in town I have not been to a cocktail party nor a club nor a private dinner without someone coming to me and saying, 'Fred, is this true, what they're saying about Mammon?' "

"Can you be more precise?" Bognor's impressions of this man were in disarray. "Who do 'they' think the main suspect is?"

"There isn't any agreement over that. No such luck. Sometimes it's Harrison. Sometimes it's Cernik and Eleanor. Sometimes Dolores."

"But never Prideaux or Amos Littlejohn."

"If it were I wouldn't be worrying. The company can live with either of those two being guilty. But if it's another board member we're in trouble."

"What about you?"

"No one has quite had the gall to point the finger at me in my presence," he said, "though they have come close."

"And what am *I* supposed to do about it?"

Crombie helped himself to a dollop of mustard. "We must have a solution," he said. "I don't care who it is but we need to have the whole deal wrapped up and out of the way. If the RCMP won't nail Prideaux because of the political situation then it will just have to be somebody else."

"Irrespective of whether they did it or not."

"Sure. Provided the charge sticks."

Bognor had decided. His first impression had let him down. This man was by no means nice. As nasty in his way as Baker. At least Baker was hot-blooded. Bognor wondered about Crombie's sex life with La Bandanna. He would have to talk to La Bandanna, though not, perhaps about Colonel Crombie's bodily functions. For the time being however Bognor decided to play ball.

"Let's assume," he said, abandoning the steak and kidney, "that Prideaux is out of the question because of politics. Let's further assume that Smith is right and that he did it. What then?"

"Find someone else."

"Even if they're innocent?"

"I already said that."

"Isn't that a little . . . immoral?"

Crombie too laid down his knife and fork. "Listen to me," he said. "You and I have been around. We know that there are times when an individual has to be sacrificed for the greater good. I agree that it would be neater and tidier if we could pin this rap on the right guy, but we have to live with the reality of the situation. If we can't do it to the right guy we'll have to find a scapegoat."

Bognor frowned.

"Don't be so scrupulous," said Colonel Crombie silkily. "Provided we find a good lawyer the guy will only get a few years. There'll be plenty of mitigating circumstances, and remission for good behaviour. He'll be out again in a few years. And Canadian penitentiaries are fine, civilized places. Okay, so it's not perfect, but it has to be done."

"Have anyone in mind?" enquired Bognor dryly, but Crombie did not seem to notice the irony. Or if he did he was not letting on. "I'm sorry about the food," he said, "they must have changed chef. The coffee's okay, though. Come and have some coffee and a brandy to take away the taste. We'll find somewhere really quiet."

In the elevator Crombie said he had been to see the Leafs play a couple of nights back. He had been shocked at the ineptitude of their performance but disturbed, too, to find that even in Maple Leaf Gardens he had run into old friends who had got wind of the bad vibes coming out of Mammon HQ. It was only a matter of time, said Crombie, before the press did start running speculative stories, and once that happened shares would really start to dip. Right now the talk was confined to makers and shakers in Rosedale and Westmount. Once the gossip filtered into the *Globe* and *Maclean's* it would be on the little-old-lady circuit. People owned Mammon shares even in Lethbridge, Alberta, and Cape Breton, and they'd sell the second they got wind of what was being alleged.

"Okay," said Bognor, as they sat in the remotest corner of the smoking room, yards from the twitching ears of the nearest potential eavesdropper. "Shoot."

Crombie pulled out a pipe and spent a minute or so lighting it. He smoked Sobranie, its vanilla smell wafting across to Bognor in a series of blue storm clouds.

"My information," said Crombie, now very conspiratorial, "is that Farquhar was killed with a solution in his bath oil which combined with the water in his bath to give off some form of toxic gas."

Bognor nodded.

"Am I right?"

"More or less. I'm not a chemist. But that's the essence of the matter. As it were."

Crombie did not even flicker in recognition of the pun. Perhaps he considered it tasteless, though how he could think anything

Newark Public Library
Newark, New York 14513

tasteless beside what he was suggesting Bognor could scarcely imagine.

"In which case anyone who could lay his hands on one of those bottles would be able to uncork it, put the solution in, recork and get it into Farquhar's bathroom or into Littlejohn's reserve stock."

"In theory."

"The real problem would be getting a hold of one of those bottles."

Bognor said nothing, but waited.

"You'll know by now that several of us were given bottles as a Christmas present."

"Yes."

"That's more than Smith of the Mounties knew."

"Or cared," said Bognor.

"So you have a fair number of plausible suspects."

"Did you have bath oil for Christmas?"

"Oh, yes. Dolores too. And Harrison."

"Are you telling me that I should just pick one or other of you out of a hat?"

"Not quite." Crombie fiddled with his pipe. "Some of us have more compelling motives than others. I, for instance, made no secret of my dislike for Farquhar but I'd learned to live with it. Nothing new about it. If I was going to kill him I'd have done it thirty years ago or more."

"And your friend, Dolores?"

"Same thing. She had a great deal more reason to kill him when they were living together. He treated her abominably. Also she was well looked after. He paid her a handsome pension and he bought her the apartment in Manhattan as well as the house in Saratoga."

"Who then?"

Crombie sucked hard on the stem of his pipe. Smoke rose in puffs the size of men's hands.

"Have you talked to Ainsley Cernik?"

"Not yet."

"I think you should."

"I appreciate the advice. Are you going to be more specific? Or am I to find out for myself?"

"I'll suggest one or two thoughts. You know Cernik's background history?"

"I'd like to hear it from you."

"Okay. Cernik came out of Czechoslovakia in sixty-eight. He's from Prague. Claims to have been some sort of dissident leader, a freethinking liberal who was on the Russians' blacklist because of his outspoken views. All that junk. They all say that. Frankly I don't believe a word of it. I've talked to one or two other émigrés who knew him in the old days and they all say Ainsley swam with the tide and bent with the wind. He was big in the black market. He had a garage downtown somewhere, used to service the official Tatra cars for the government ministries and some of the embassies too. That gave him all sorts of useful entrees and he was into everything—booze, dope, girls, gasoline—the lot. My information is that he was a casualty of the Prague Spring, not the Russian invasion. They say he actually came out while Dubček was still in charge."

"Why didn't he go to Russia if that's where his friends were?"

"Oh, there wasn't anything ideological about Cernik's Russian friendships. He's always been a chancer, a natural capitalist. If there was money in it Cernik would sell his wife, his mother, his daughters, maybe even himself. No future in the Soviet Union for that sort of entrepreneur."

"I take it you're not too keen on Mr. Cernik."

Crombie shrugged. "Easy come, easy go. I liked Farquhar in a way. Cernik's a shit but I'd sooner have an entertaining shit than a tight-arsed saint, if you'll forgive the expression."

"So Cernik played the black market in Czechoslovakia, and then he came here."

Crombie picked up the story. "Yeah. He came here and went straight into the secondhand-car business, made a neat little fortune and was bought out by one of the smaller Mammon subsidiaries. Farquhar spotted him. He was on the main board inside six months. And a year later they started to fight."

"What did they fight about?"

"Eleanor to begin with. Only child. You know what men are like about only children. Particularly an only girl. Even more par-

ticularly when the mother died giving birth. Farquhar was obses-
sive about Eleanor. Indecently so."

"Farquhar tried to stop her marrying Cernik?"

"They fought over Eleanor and Cernik won out. Inevitable."

"If Cernik won out then I don't see why he had a motive for
killing Farquhar. The other way round, maybe."

"That was only the beginning," said Crombie. "From then on
they fought about everything. We all fought with Farquhar in our
different ways, but usually we saw the commercial sense of
what he was doing even if we didn't like the way he did it. Most
of us were too greedy to make real trouble and most of the time
he was right. We all did well from Farquhar's decisions."

"Including Cernik?"

"Including Cernik. But that didn't stop him fighting. And
gradually he began to win some support. Younger guys were
coopted on to the board. He said that Farquhar was flying by the
seat of his pants, taking decisions based on hunches when they
ought to be based on proper market surveys and analyses and
God knows what all. Most of us, particularly the older ones, we
were prepared to back Farquhar's hunches against any number of
statistical analyses but around the mid-seventies we started getting some new blood in: men in their late thirties and early forties
with degrees in business studies from Harvard. They sided with
Cernik."

Bognor nodded. He wished sometimes that there could be an
influx of new blood into the Board of Trade to support him in
the unending battle with Parkinson.

"That's still no more of a motive than anyone else's," he said.
"Especially if he was beginning to win, and it sounds as if he
was."

"You forget," said Crombie, "Cernik was powerful and clever
and he married the boss's daughter, but he still had less than ten
per cent of the shares. Farquhar had a controlling interest all his
life."

"I see." Bognor did indeed begin to see. "And when he died
Eleanor was to inherit the lot, so that she would be the most
powerful single figure in Mammoncorp."

"Right." Crombie leaned back and jabbed at Bognor with his

pipe. "Now even though Farquhar was upset by Eleanor marrying Cernik he was still besotted with her. There was no way he was going to cut her out of his will, specially as there was no other kith and kin. Cernik banked on this and he overstepped the mark. There was no one deal in particular but he took Farquhar on once too often and finally Farquhar couldn't take any more. He had Eleanor in and said that if her husband didn't toe the line then he would disinherit her. He wouldn't cut her out altogether. There would be cash and property but very definitely no Mammon shares. She was given six weeks to talk him round and if she didn't do it, then it was going to be a new will and Cernik's chance of taking over at Mammon right out the window."

"When was all this? This confrontation between Farquhar and Eleanor."

"That's just it," said Crombie, softly. "It happened almost exactly six weeks before Farquhar died."

"And do we know whether Eleanor did persuade Cernik to cool down?"

"'We' may, but *I* don't."

"And who told you all this?"

Crombie hesitated for a while. "Dolores," he said, at last. "She remained very close to Farquhar after they split. He confided in her a great deal."

"And she in you?"

"Yes." Crombie smiled a soft superior smile. "And she in me."

CHAPTER 10

It was not easy to agitate Monica. She had the rather bloody-minded sangfroid that one associates with the better sort of memsahib, an indifference verging on disdain for those who attempted to make her life difficult. These ranged from tax inspectors to taxi drivers and included most foreigners, especially those living abroad, practically all shop assistants and all cloakroom attendants. This attitude frightened some people to whom she appeared hard and even, it was sometimes alleged, "bitchy." She had once frightened off a would-be rapist on Hampstead Heath by advancing on him waving her umbrella and shouting fearful obscenities. The man had turned and run, leading Bognor to remark superciliously that he did not think he had been a potential rapist but simply a harmless flasher trying to make someone take an interest in him. Whatever the truth of the matter the story had gone the rounds so that when her name was mentioned people would say, "Oh, yes, isn't she the woman who attacked the rapist?" This was unfair, but not wholly so.

When, therefore, Bognor lurched down the corridor of the hotel and managed to press the doorbell with his forehead—his reliance on crutches meaning that he did not have a hand free to deal with it in the normal manner—he was surprised to find that Monica had put the door on the chain and at first refused to open.

"Who is it?" she called, suspiciously.

Bognor put his eye up to the peephole in the middle of the door and peered in. It was quite dark.

"Stand back from the door." Monica's voice sounded shaky. "I can't see who it is if you don't stand back."

"I can't stand back. I'll fall over. I'm leaning against the door. I'm on crutches."

"Who is it? Will you please move back?"

"Monica. It's me. Simon. Your husband. Let me in."

"Simon! Is that you?"

"Yes. It's me. What's up? Let me in." This was peculiar. Most unlike Monica.

"Hang on."

He heard bolts being shot. Then the door was pulled back a few inches, causing him to stumble against it.

"Careful," he shouted angrily. He had stubbed his toe, which protruded from the plaster and was covered only in gauze and bandage. Moreover, he was in danger of falling completely if the door was opened any more. "Wait a sec," he shouted but she did not hear in time and opened the door to its full extent whereupon he did fall, like a pine tree under the axe, straight into his wife's arms. She staggered back but clung on and together they tottered into the room locked together, before finally collapsing on the bed in a heap. He lay still, surprisingly unhurt by the tumble, "Hello," he said, staring into his wife's eyes. He was surprised to see that they were brown. He knew that they were brown, of course. Or had known and forgotten. Or seldom thought about it. Or hardly ever looked to check. "Hello, brown eyes," he said, kissing her nose.

"Thank heaven you're back," she said. "Hang on." She extricated herself and hurried to the door. Bognor sat up and watched with disbelief as she bolted it and reattached the chain.

"Whatever's the matter?" he asked, beginning to catch her concern. She looked uncharacteristically flustered. Her hair, usually immaculately mousey, was a mess, her face blotchy.

She sat down in the armchair, perching on the edge. "Have you got a cigarette?" she asked.

"Of course not. You know I don't smoke cigarettes. I've got a panatella. Quite a thin one. Cuban I think."

She shook her head, stood and went to the window.

"Do you mind if I have a drink?" She was staring down at the city streets below, hands sunk deep in the pockets of her skirt.

"Of course not. Isn't there some of your duty-free left?"

"I feel like brandy actually."

"Okay. I'll ring room service. Or would you rather go down to the bar?"

"The bar won't serve alcohol in midafternoon. Anyway, I'd rather not go out if you don't mind."

Bognor pulled himself up awkwardly and dialled room service on the bedside phone. "Look, what is all this?" he asked, quite peevish now.

She waited until he had ordered the brandy. Two brandies in fact. Then she said, "I had a phone call."

"Ah." Bognor grinned. "I know you don't enjoy telephone calls but I can't help feeling you're rather overdoing the reaction."

"Don't be flippant. It was an anonymous phone call."

"A heavy breather? A Canadian heavy breather? Or a British breather?"

His heavy flippancy coaxed a timid half smile but it evaporated at once.

"Worse than that," she said, pushing back a stray strand of hair. "He was threatening us."

"He? Who?"

"I don't know who. He was anonymous. He didn't give a name. Oh, where's that brandy?" She sat down again and then stood immediately.

"But what did he *say*?" Bognor was exasperated. Try as he might he could not understand Monica's anguish. She was usually so level-headed. She was the only one of them who could stand the sight of blood, who did not flinch from the dentist.

"He threatened us. Both of us. You in particular."

"Oh, for heaven's sake. I'm always being threatened. What would life be without threats?"

"I wish you'd be serious."

The doorbell rang. Monica went to answer it, peering with exaggerated care through the spy-hole. "It's okay," she said to Bognor. "It's the drinks."

"Okay," said Bognor. "So it's the drinks. So let him in."

"Are you sure it is?" she said, hesitating with the chain. "It could be a trick."

"For God's sake." He seized a crutch and swung himself up into a standing position, where he remained briefly and uncertainly before thinking better of it and subsiding once more onto the bed. "Let him in. If it's an assassin I'll hit him with a crutch. Be your age."

She let him in. The youth, a slim Thai of about fifteen, looked at them apprehensively. Monica followed him across the room one hand held very stiff in the position she had learned at evening classes in karate the previous year. Bognor had not been impressed with her karate, which she had practised on him from time to time with ambiguous results. Bognor signed the cheque and Monica followed the bewildered waiter out of the room peering down the corridor to left and right before reentering and rebolting. Then she picked up the glass and took a large slug of brandy. She gasped slightly. "That's better," she said.

"Please explain," said Bognor, not very sympathetically, "why you're in such a state?"

"Because he could see me."

"*See* you?"

Now Bognor *was* concerned. He too drank a deepish draught of alcohol. "How do you know he could see you?"

"Because he told me."

"Be sensible."

Monica sucked in her bottom lip and chewed on it for a second. Then, choosing the words with care she said, "He described everything I was wearing."

"That's not difficult," said Bognor, nervously. "Inspired guesswork. You usually wear a skirt and a shirt."

"He told me the colours and the patterns. He described my earrings. He knew you were out. He knew what time you left. He knew I'd had a room service lunch. He could *see* me."

"Maybe he'd seen you outside."

"I haven't been out of the room all day. I had a bath and I've been reading. The only way he could possibly know what I was wearing was by looking in through the window."

"Maybe it was the boy who brought you lunch. Or maybe he bribed the boy who brought you lunch."

"I thought of that," said Monica, "but it doesn't make it any better."

"I suppose not." Bognor swilled the brandy round in his glass and wished he had a clearer head. "What did he say?"

"That we must leave. Within forty-eight hours at the latest. Otherwise there would be more trouble and this time it would be worse than just a beating up. He said it would be perfectly possible to shoot us through the window of our room."

"Now that," said Bognor emphatically, "*is* being melodramatic."

"If he can see into our room, why shouldn't he shoot into our room?"

"Anything else?"

"I should have thought that was enough."

"What did he sound like?"

Monica thought for a moment, frowning. "He didn't sound like anything much. I got the impression he was disguising his voice somehow. Probably talking through a handkerchief. He was quite indistinct."

"Canadian?"

"Yes. Certainly not English anyway."

Bognor went to the window and gazed out. It was a grey day but clear. The reef of islands were clearly visible with the opaque waters of the lake stretching away towards a horizon which was indistinct, so nearly did the colour of the water match the colour of the sky. To his left he saw Ward's Island with a ferry chugging busily towards its landing stage, a precisely etched V of wake fanning out behind it. He was reminded of Louise, felt a sharp guilty pang of loss. She had not been in touch since the hospital visit.

"It was a man?" he said, not turning round.

"Of course," Monica sounded impatient.

"I'm sorry. I just wondered. Through the handkerchief. You know. One could be mistaken."

"It was a man."

They were about a quarter of a mile, maybe more, from the lake shore. Between them and the water was the main railway line. Montreal to the left, Vancouver to the right. It was from down there, from the bowels of that slablike piece of colonial

gothick that the Spirit of Saskatoon had set out on its last fatal
voyage to Winnipeg and beyond. Bognor pressed his nose to the
glass and let his thoughts wander along the track. A double-
decker "go" train in green-and-white livery came sliding in from
the direction of Missisauga, past a parked caterpillar of dome
cars, waiting to make the long journey west.

"I'll bet this glass is bulletproof," he said, breathing on it and
watching it mist over. Behind him Monica said nothing. He
looked down at the streets. He could see people walking about,
unhurried in that purposeful yet unfrantic way that Canadians
affected, but he could not even sex them let alone describe their
clothing or their dress. He could barely distinguish the colours
of the cars, yet his eyesight was A-1. If the anonymous caller
was phoning from ground level there was no way he could
possibly have made out what Monica was wearing. He looked
around him. There were about half a dozen buildings as high as
their hotel. Most of them were office buildings. A man with
binoculars or a telescope would probably be able to see into the
hotel rooms from any of them. That would, presumably, mean
that he worked in one of them. It would be possible to get
a list through Smith of the Mounties, but laborious and time-con-
suming. Scarcely worth it. The only building open to the public
was the CN Tower. It was primarily a communications building
but there was a restaurant at the top, and two viewing platforms.
Bognor had not been up yet. Nor was he sure he wanted to. He
was inclined to vertigo, and as he watched the tiny lifts crawl up
the outside of the futuristic concrete folly he felt his stomach
turn. The view must be fantastic . . .

"Got it," he said. "The CN Tower. The viewing platform.
They must have telescopes or something up there. That's where
he was. Look!"

She came to the window and peered across at "the world's
tallest free-standing building." "You could be right," she said.

"Let's go and check." He felt exhilarated. "We ought to have a
look before we leave. And if we're leaving in forty-eight hours we
may not have another chance."

Monica hesitated. "Suppose he's there," she said. "Suppose he
does something."

"Well, then, dear, we'll have to play it by ear. But he's given us forty-eight hours. Besides which he's hardly likely to do anything very conspicuous in the city's most popular tourist attraction. It is rather public."

"So was the zoo." She said it acidly. He could not remember when she was so agitated. It must be marriage.

"You think it's Baker again, do you?" he asked.

"I don't know." From the tone of her voice she didn't care much either. But she agreed to come at last, despite her misgivings. Just as they had drunk the dregs of the brandy and Monica had finished some perfunctory titivating, the phone rang. She refused to answer so Bognor, creaking and swearing under his breath, lowered himself onto the bed and took the call.

"Hi, Si." Bognor sighed inwardly. How he disliked stupidity in others. It was bad enough in oneself, but he had almost come to terms with that. Confronted with a similar affliction in someone else he was relentlessly unforgiving.

"It's Pete Smith," said Pete Smith.

"Hello," said Bognor, coolly.

"How ya doin?"

Bognor thought he could hear the gum being flicked backwards and forwards from the right to left molars. "Quite well, thanks."

"Bones healing?"

"Yes, thank you. Bones healing very well."

"Say, Si. Guess I should warn you we just had a call about you from some French bastard."

"Oh, who?"

"Can't be one hundred per cent certain, Si, but I have my ideas. This guy is dangerous, Si. We think maybe you should have some protection."

"Protection?"

"Sure. No problem. I can send a guy right over."

"Surely that won't be necessary?"

"I'd sure as hell feel a lot happier, Si. This French bastard sounded kinda, you know, like *mean*."

"What did he say exactly?"

"I don't recall precisely what his words were Si, but his message was that if you aren't out of the country in two days then he's gonna have another go at you. Only this time he ain't gonna be so gentle. French bastard!"

"Are you sure he was French?"

"Sure he was French."

"Funny thing is, my wife had a call from someone who sounds like the same person. She said it was impossible to work out what sort of accent he had because, a, he was talking through a scarf or handkerchief and, b, he was disguising his voice."

"Listen, Si. You been here as long as I have and you learn to tell the difference between a French bastard's voice and a Canadian bastard's voice. And I'm telling you this sonofabitch was a French bastard."

"If you say so." Bognor caught Monica's eyes, raised his own heavenwards and made circular movements with his spare hand, thus indicating his extreme irritation with Smith of the RCMP.

"Okay, Si, so take care, and I'm sending one of our best men right over."

"Well, actually, we're on our way out at the moment."

"Can't you just wait a moment or two? How far ya goin'?"

"I'm only taking my wife over to the CN Tower to see the view. We'll come straight back."

"Right on, Si. Our man'll be there when you get back. Mind how you go now. Don't fall off, eh?" And the Mountie chortled happily at his joke. Bognor humoured him by saying, in his most amused and agreeable manner, "I'll try not to," then replaced the receiver with a protracted groan.

"Let's go," he said. And they went.

He shut his eyes after the first few feet, terrified by the speed at which they shot away from the ground. The lift rattled and swayed as it climbed the concrete side of the tower and the operator regaled them with a parroted spiel of meaningless statistics. They were travelling at God knows how many feet per second to a height of God knows what. God knew why. Bognor's palms were sweating. His stomach was heaving vacuum and his throat was dry. He tried swallowing. No good. He tried puffing his cheeks out and blowing. Still no good. He would have held his nose and blown but that would have meant letting go of a crutch. Not a good idea.

"Do look, darling," said Monica. "It really is a fantastic view."

"Thank you, Monica." He blew out his cheeks forlornly. "You know views upset me unless my feet are on the ground."

"You look like a hamster," she said.

After what seemed like the longest hour of his life but was probably nearer a minute, they arrived at their destination. He swung out onto the observation deck.

"There is another deck, higher up," said Monica. "Shall we try that?"

"We're high enough," said Bognor with feeling, "and we're here for a purpose. Remember." He felt better now, for the deck seemed solid. It did not sway, and there was a reassuring carpet on the floor. Also telescopes.

"Aha!" he exclaimed, pleased with his deductive processes. "I was right."

Together they moved round the circular platform until they reached a point from which they could see their hotel.

"Looks awfully small," mused Bognor, gazing down at the neat symmetrical grid sprawling away to the north. Monica slipped a quarter into the slot in the side of the grey metal telescope as requested by the instructions. Bognor bent down and put his eye to the hole. "Can't see a blind thing," he complained after a few seconds of peering.

"It's pointing straight at the hotel." Monica adjusted the machine a little to the left. "In fact I should say we're aiming almost directly at our room. Twenty-fifth floor, aren't we?"

"Yes. But I can't see anything. Ridiculous machine. It must be out of order." He pressed his eye even more tightly against the aperture. "No," he protested after another abortive peer. "Nix. Nothing. *Niente.* Just doesn't work.

The viewing platform was a turntable and it was revolving slowly. Monica readjusted the telescope to take account of the movement. "Let me try," she said, shoving at him none too gently.

"There's no point," he said. "It's out of order. Waste of twenty-five cents. You won't be able to see a thing."

"Good grief!" she said. "You must be blind as a bat. You certainly missed something."

"What do you mean?" Bognor protested. "It's out of order. You're having me on. What can you see?"

"Love in the afternoon," said Monica, not removing her eye, "In glorious Technicolor. You can see her appendix scar . . . Good heavens! They must be fit. I shouldn't like to try that."

Bognor was outraged. "Here!" he said. "Let me have a look." He grabbed at the machine, and jammed his eye to it again in the prescribed manner. "I still can't . . ." he began, and then, "Oh, wait. I see. Got it. Now wait a minute. There's a chap writing letters in here. It's a *very* clear picture. No wonder our heavy breathing Froggo could describe what you were wearing. Now where's this orgy?" He moved the telescope to left and right in an effort to locate the "XX" bedroom scene. "Ah!" he said after a few moments. "Got it! Gosh, that looks fun. Oh, hell!" The whirring sound which had begun as soon as the money was put in had come to a stop. The screen went blank.

"Got another twenty-five?" he asked.

"Certainly not." She simulated outrage. "And even if I had I wouldn't let you have it. Filthy beast. You've made your point. You *can* see into the hotel rooms from here, now leave them alone."

Bognor grinned. "Oh, all right," he said. "Where do you imagine he phoned from?" He gazed round, then located a rank of call boxes only about twenty yards away. "That's solved that, then!" he exclaimed, satisfied.

"For what it's worth." She had gone broody again. "It's like the murder itself. You know *how* it was done. You have about half a dozen alternative why's and absolutely no idea about who. Same with this. Man comes up here, spies on me in our room, phones through a warning, putting the fear of God into me by seeming to be omniscient. Clever idea and it had the desired effect. But who and why?"

"He's presumably alarmed because he thinks I'm onto him." Bognor felt self-important. "He's got the wind up."

"Not half as much as I have." Monica spoke with feeling. "The only consoling thought is how wrong he is. You're not onto anybody. Whatever makes him think you are? How did he know where to look?"

"Must have had our room number," said Bognor thoughtfully.

"He's obviously more perceptive than we realize."

"By further than we think."

"Quite."

They both laughed at this. There were several other tourists milling around the deck, also a school party inadequately controlled by a very young, very stout schoolmistress. The children were running around the place, clambering over the telescopes, thumping each other from time to time, shouting, fooling, having a good time. It was difficult to feel threatened among such a group.

"Coming down?" asked Bognor. "Or are you venturing onward and upward?"

"I've seen enough" she said. "More than enough." She giggled. "How mortifying to be spied on like those two. I wonder how many other people saw them?"

"They should have drawn the curtains," replied Bognor.

There was no queue when they arrived at the entrance to the down elevator, and the door was already open.

"After you," said Bognor, mock graciously. She grinned back. They both felt relieved. Euphoric even.

"What, no operator?" asked Bognor as the door closed behind them. They were the only two on board.

"They probably only have them on the ascent." Monica took a couple of paces and pressed up against the outer glass wall. "It really is rather incredible," she said, as they began to fall. "We're over a mile high. Or are we? Can that be right?"

"I wish you'd come away from that door. It's fantastically flimsy." Bognor leaned back against the solid wall behind him, the wall which pressed against the tower's reassuringly dense core. "I hate it," he said, shutting his eyes. "Do come away."

She moved back towards him, telling him not to be an old woman. As she did the little cubicle slowed, then came to a halt and hung there high above the railroad tracks and the lake, swing-

ing gently. Below them an aeroplane took off from the island airport and passed, straining for height, some hundreds of feet
below them. "Are we almost there?" pleaded Bognor, not looking
out from eyes screwed tight from fear.

"Not really." Monica's voice was tense, self-consciously assured.
"We've obviously stopped to admire the view."

Bognor opened an eye gingerly. "Good heavens," he exclaimed,
"we're miles high. Is there an alarm? For God's sake let's press
it."

"It's perfectly all right." Monica was back to her normal self.
Bognor gave her courage, not by being courageous but by de-
manding reassurance and strength. He had always brought out
the universal aunt in her and the charm was working as usual.
They were well suited.

"Well, what are we going to do?" he asked. "We can't just sit
here."

They were too high to be able to see people. Even the cars on
Lakeshore Boulevard and the Gardiner were no more than dots.

Suddenly the car jerked and fell downwards for perhaps five
seconds, stopping as suddenly as it had begun, hanging once more
in space, swinging gently.

Somewhere someone laughed.

The laughter came from above and for a second Bognor had a
manic thought that there was a man clinging to the elevator's
roof, lying there giggling softly at their plight.

"Tannoy," said Monica. "There's a loudspeaker set in the ceiling."

"We should never have come out," moaned Bognor. "It was a
trap."

Through the loudspeaker system came words, muffled, and
peculiarly enunciated as if the speaker was disguising his natural
manner of speech.

"No machinery is foolproof," said the voice. "One minor mal-
function would send you to an unpleasant end. And it's so easy to
throw a switch."

There was a creak. A sudden lurch. Their little cell plummet-
ted again, falling for an eternity. Monica screamed.

Once more they stopped and hung in space.

"There is a telephone. Next to the emergency call. You could pick up the receiver and talk to me if you wished. I can't, however, promise to answer your questions. But feel free. Feel perfectly free." The voice clicked out.

"Not bloody likely," said Bognor, who seemed to have tapped some reserves of courage, though he still kept his eyes tightly closed. He was not a natural coward, particularly when confronted with a human adversary, even one who was speaking to him disembodied on the other end of a telephone line. It was the vertigo which upset him and he could very nearly come to terms with that if he remained blind.

"Very well." The voice resumed. It was flat, monotone, without any clue to personality. Monica was crying softly. "I am not going to kill you," the voice continued. "Not yet. I'm showing you how simple it would be. At any time. A high-velocity rifle with telescopic sights while you relax in your very own hotel room. An unexplained mishap while you make a routine tourist's visit to the sights of the city. So easy. So terribly, terribly easy. And so very avoidable. All you have to do is leave Canada by midnight tomorrow. Then you can live on untroubled. If not . . ."

There was another creaking, a horrid pause and then a descent which sent the pit of Bognor's stomach to his mouth and made him gasp for breath. Monica clung onto him, her fingernails biting into the thick cloth of his jacket, as she fought to bring her terror under control.

"Please, God, make him stop!" she screamed.

There was another crash. They stopped again and hung, swinging and suspended once again. There was another soft chuckle on the Tannoy and then, mercifully, they started to descend again, more slowly this time, until seconds later they reached terra firma and walked out to freedom and the illusion, at least, of safety.

A few steps from the exit they found an upholstered bench seat onto which they subsided. For some five minutes they sat there, silent. Bognor found that sweat was dripping saltily into his eyes. Monica was shaking and unable to control it. He grasped her hand and she returned the pressure gratefully. At length he said: "Shall we go?"

She nodded. "Back to the hotel now. And back to England to-morrow. I've never been so frightened in my life."

"No." Bognor was angry now that the danger had, if only temporarily, evaporated. "It is perfectly bloody to involve you too. It's nothing to do with you."

She smiled. "You are my husband. Aren't we supposed to share everything in these emancipated times? Surely that includes risks. Women's lib wouldn't want you to hog all the danger."

"Who do you think it was?"

"God knows." She grimaced. "It could have been the same voice I heard on the phone but honestly I couldn't be sure. That Tannoy thing has such a dehumanizing effect. It could have been anyone. What do you think? Would you recognize it?"

Bognor shook his head. "No," he said, "I can't think I would. It certainly didn't begin to remind me of anyone I've met out here. Whoever it was must have friends in the control room."

"I thought of that," agreed Monica. "Do you think the Quebecois conspiracy idea does stand up?"

"And the CN Tower elevators are in the hands of the Quebecois? It's possible, but scarcely likely."

"What happened is scarcely likely. We could have been killed, Simon."

He nodded. "But it's just as likely that that psychopath Johnny Baker infiltrated the control room. Or any of our other suspects, come to that. Presumably everyone has their price and when all's said and done they were just fooling around. It could have been passed off as a practical joke."

"Some joke."

"Yes. But." Bognor sighed. For enough money it would almost certainly have been possible to arrange the complicity of the very few key personnel necessary. Especially if they could be convinced that no serious harm was intended.

They had reached the end of the long walkway which led from the base of the tower to Front Street. Emerging onto the sidewalk they both as if by instinct turned to look up at the top of the tower. Even looking *up* at the monster made Bognor feel dizzy. Above the revolving platforms the lights blinked out from the great needle which pointed to the sky. Along the tower's huge grey concrete side a yellow elevator crawled upwards like some inexorable insect. Bognor shuddered and looked down at his feet. "I'm not going up there again," he said.

CHAPTER 11

They found their new guard waiting for them at the hotel. He was at least six foot four and big with it. He was wearing a standard-issue Tip Top Tailor's suit which bulged with ill-concealed muscle and firearm, also a fixed grin which twitched as he chewed the inevitable gum. Alongside him by the reception desk was Bognor's old sparring partner Pete Smith.

"Hi, Si!" he said, secreting his gum in a corner of the mouth not necessary for speech. "Good to see you, Mrs. Bognor. I'd like you to meet Gary." He indicated the young giant at his side. "Gary once had a trial for the Toronto Argonauts and has a black belt in karate. He is trained to kill. Like, I mean, *kill.*"

"Hello there, Mrs. Bognor." Gary grinned yet more broadly, displaying an impressive array of killer teeth, and shook hands.

"Hi, Mr. Bognor, sir," and he seized Bognor's somewhat flabby hand in his enormous nutcracker grip. Bognor winced.

"Hello, Gary," he said. "Please call me Simon. Well, call me Si if you prefer."

"And I'm Monica," said Monica. "But not Mon, if you don't mind."

They all laughed weakly.

"How was the view, Mrs. Bognor?" enquired Smith of the Mounties, politely.

Monica put a hand to her temple and attempted a smile. "Spectacular," she said, "but not without its little excitements."

"We had a bit of an adventure as a matter of fact," conceded Simon. "The lift got stuck."

The two Mounties glanced at one another incomprehendingly.

"The lift, Si? Stuck?" Smith was at sea.

"Sorry. Elevator. We were left hanging around rather a lot. In midair. I have a bad head for heights."

"Jeez, that's too bad. I heard they sometimes have trouble with those elevators. They were manufactured in Japan."

"Do you mind if we sit down for a moment?" asked Monica. She had gone an unnatural pinkish grey. "I don't feel awfully well."

"Oh, say, sure. Hey, why didn't you say so, Mrs. Bognor. Let's find a chair. Gary, fetch Mrs. Bognor a glass of water." Smith sprung to life. Obviously a man for a crisis. He put an arm round Monica in a manly grasp and helped her towards the bar, where a willowy girl in a low-cut evening gown was showing guests to their tables. In seconds they were seated in a corner. Monica had a glass of ice with a little water in it and they were confronted with long slim cards explaining the infinite variety of cocktails on offer.

"That's quite all right," Monica kept saying. "I feel a lot better thank you. Yes, really. It was just a passing thing. I felt a bit faint, that's all."

"Delayed shock," said Bognor, who was feeling a touch of the delayed shocks himself.

The Mounties fussed around awhile and then ordered a brace of Harvey Wallbangers while the Bognors settled for double brandies. Then Bognor explained what had happened.

"Jeez," said Smith, when he had finished. He hit his palm several times with a clenched fist. "I will nail that French bastard! I will nail him, no matter what. No matter what, I will nail him, so help me. Those bastards in Ottawa gonna have to play ball. This isn't just a political affair any longer, this is threatening to kill a member of the British Board of Trade and a guest in this great country of ours."

Bognor did not wish to become involved in yet another argument about French bastards. Besides, he was feeling confused about murders and threats to murder, and he was inclined to accept that the French bastard theory was as likely as the Colonel Crombie-Bandanna Rose theory or the Harrison Bentley theory or the Johnny Baker theory or any of the other theories which he was no nearer standing up. The most maddening aspect of the case was that the guilty party clearly believed that Bognor was onto him.

Bognor said this. Or something like it.

"He is a frightened man, Si." Smith took a draught of Wallbanger and wiped his regulation neatly clipped Mountie moustache with a paper napkin. "That is one frightened man. That's what makes me mad. That's what bugs me. That man is frightened. He is a cornered rat and a cornered rat is a dangerous beast, Si. That cornered rat has to be put away, but his friends in Ottawa just aren't letting me do that. And so he is out on the run, a menace to society. He is not safe to be on the streets. You know that? The politicans are letting him roam the streets threatening law-abiding citizens who are going about their lawful business. It's the politicans who are ruining this damn country. If the Soviets nuked Ottawa they'd be doing the rest of us a favour, you know that?"

He drank more Wallbanger.

"I think it might be best if we were to catch a plane back to Britain tomorrow." said Bognor. "I'd rather not be killed. And I'd much rather my wife wasn't."

"I don't like to hear that," said Smith. "Mean to say, Gary here will shoot on sight. On sight. There is no way any harm is going to come to you good people."

Bognor nodded his appreciation. "All the same," he said, "I don't think you should be shooting at people on our behalf. And I'm really not doing any good here. You're obviously well under control and there's nothing I can do to help. And I'm wanted back at the office."

"If you say so, Si." Bognor recognized that the policeman would be quite happy to see the back of him, but he was impressed by his scrupulous politeness.

"Tell me, Si." Smith suddenly came over expansive. "Do you still think Farquhar was killed by someone else? I mean you can be straight with me. Shoot from the hip."

"As a matter of fact"—Bognor rotated his glass and watched the amber alcohol lap the sides of the balloon—"I'm not convinced, but I have no proof that it was anyone else, and I have no evidence to suggest that it *wasn't* our French friend."

"Hmmm." Smith nodded his head several times, pursed his lips and pinched his moustache. "Can't say fairer than that," he said eventually.

"Just one thing though," Bognor added. "Well, two actually. First I want to have a word with the Cerniks before I leave. I'll try to set that up for tomorrow. I really need to establish his intentions for Mammon as much as discuss the murder. Trade matter, you understand . . ."

Smith nodded. "Sure, sure," he said.

"And then I thought I'd make one visit when I return to London."

"Oh, yeah?"

"I hear that Farquhar was not at all a well man. In fact he was very sick. He had several bits and pieces taken out of him over the last few years, and he was always junked up to the eyebrows with pills. It seems he had no faith in his Canadian doctor and went to a quack in Harley Street."

"Harley Street?"

"London. It's where the expensive doctors hang out."

Smith shrugged. "You go see who you like, Si," he said. "Can't say I see any future in finding out how ill a man was when he's dead. Like suppose he did have the Big C, those French bastards got to him first, eh?"

Bognor grinned. "I'll still go and see him," he said. "You never know. It doesn't do to leave a stone unturned. Or so I've found in the past."

"Lookit, Si." Smith drained his glass of Wallbanger. "You just carry on and do your own thing, and let me know what you find out. And Gary will stay with you until you're safely up, up and away and flying back home again. Okay. So long." He rose, brushed down his trousers and shook hands. "Good seeing you guys. See you again soon. Have a good flight."

Monica and Simon watched him shamble off through the swing doors, waved a last farewell, and went upstairs to pack. They were about to venture out for a last supper in Toronto at a highly recommended Rumanian restaurant on Yonge Street just beyond Merton and Balliol, and were wondering what to do with Gary. Monica thought they would have to invite him to share their table. Simon was for leaving him outside in the car. The argument was threatening to become acrimonious, when they heard altercation outside in the corridor.

A male voice, Gary's, saying, "Lady, I have my orders. No one is entering this room without authorization."

A female voice. "I am a friend. It's very important."

Gary was impressively unbudgeable. The lady quietly persistent.

"It's your little French friend," said Monica.

"Oh," said Bognor. "Yes. I think you may be right. Louise." He felt himself flush and was annoyed at this lack of self-control.

"Well, aren't you going to let her in?"

"Um. Yes, I suppose so. Do you think I should?"

"Well, of course. Why ever not?" Monica regarded him with incredulity.

"She is a friend of Prideaux. That 'French bastard.' She may be a villain."

"Don't be silly." The voices outside were rising. "If you won't," snapped Monica, "then I will." And she flounced to the door, unchained and unbolted it and admitted Louise, placating Gary with an assurance that all was well.

She did not look well. She was wearing jeans, tailored and expensive and creased, also a crisp white shirt, probably silk. Nothing wrong with her turn-out, nor that neat little figure, but there were dark rings under her eyes and her face was pinched, thin, more lined than he remembered.

"I'm sorry," she exclaimed, taking in Monica's little black dress and pearl earrings and, no doubt, inhaling the Chanel, recently and liberally applied. "You're going out. I won't take a moment, but I am worried and I thought I should come to you."

"Why? What is it? Sit down. Have a drink." Bognor was flapping.

"No. I won't keep you." She smiled apologetically and Bognor remembered how elfin and gamine she was. He had always had a soft spot for the French, or, more accurately, for French women.

He was still in love with Juliette Greco and Zizi Jeanmaire. Had been since the age of eight. And the Quebecois were sort of French. "It's about Maggie," she said. "She's vanished."

"Vanished? What do you mean, vanished?"

"She's gone. I don't know where she is."

"When did this happen?"

She sighed. "I'm not really sure. After . . . well, after the affair at the zoo, we drove to her place in the country. It's a cottage about a hundred miles northwest. Just a little place. She wanted to get away."

"She phoned from there that evening. When I was with her husband."

The girl nodded. "That's right. She stayed there a few nights. I spoke to her every day on the telephone."

"Didn't Baker find her there?"

"Her husband didn't know it existed. She never told him. She used it as, you know, a 'love nest.' It was where she took men." She glanced at Monica, embarrassed. "I am sorry," she said, "I don't like to say these things. She is my friend. But I think she is in trouble and it's important that you know these things, I think."

Monica smiled, a touch glacially. "I'm quite beyond surprise," she murmured, "and, for an Englishwoman, virtually shockproof. Do carry on, please."

"Then," said Louise, "she visited in New York for a few days. Seeing friends, I don't know who. Again I talked to her every day. She was okay. Then she came back two days ago. I met her at the airport. We drove to the cottage together. I left her there, and since then she has not telephoned nor has she answered the telephone. I think she is in trouble."

"Couldn't she have just done a bunk? Escaped again. Run away?"

"I don't think so, no. I am her best friend. Maybe her only friend. She tells me everything and we agreed that we would speak to each other every day. No, she would not just disappear like this unless she was in bad, deep trouble."

"Shouldn't you tell the police?"

She shook her head. "I don't like to do that. I don't trust them.

Also they don't trust me. And they will go straight to Baker, her husband, and he will say, 'Oh, don't worry, everything is all right.'"

"You think Baker has her?"

"For sure. Who else?"

"I've no idea, but if you'll forgive my saying so she seems to get around rather a lot. I mean, she's not exactly discriminating with her favours."

Louise's mouth set, firm and irritated.

"I came to you because I thought you would be sympathetic. I thought you would understand."

Bognor was upset. He had not meant to put his foot in it.

"I'm sorry," he said. "It's just that, well, it's surely possible that she's gone off with someone for a day or two to get away from everything."

"I don't think so." Louise was very cold now, her voice hostile, disillusioned. Bognor longed to be able to say something of comfort, even to put a consoling arm around her. He remembered the night of the storm, standing on the jetty, close together, waiting for the ferry that never came. He wished he wasn't so impossibly susceptible. At the moment, and just for the moment, he also wished he could not feel Monica's eyes boring into him, watching for the slightest hint that he might be wavering from the straight and narrow.

"I'm sorry," said Bognor, attempting compromise, "I'd love to help. I would really. But we fly back to England tomorrow. The fact is that Baker, or someone unknown, is still after us. Me, that is. We were given a really rather unpleasant afternoon in one of the elevators at the CN Tower."

"I'm sorry to hear it," said Louise dully. "I see now that you cannot help. I hope you have a good flight. Good-bye, Mrs. Bognor."

Monica flashed out one of her most memsahib smiles.

"I'll see you out." Bognor could not remember when he had last felt so impossibly constrained, and helpless. He swung to the door on his crutches, another fatuous gesture because it was Louise who actually opened it, leaving him hovering like a stork or crane, stiff-legged, clumsy, useless.

"How's Jean-Claude?" he tried, pseudo-brightly.

"I haven't seen him." She looked up at him. Was it his imagination, or were there tears gathering at the corners of her eyes. Her mouth was turned down at the corners, like a child's. She looked as if she might crumple at any moment.

"I am sorry," he said, softly. "Truly."

"Yes," she said, avoiding his look. "Good-bye." And very quickly she reached up and kissed him, a fleeting dab of the lips on his cheeks, turned and was gone, hurrying down the corridor towards the lifts, leaving Bognor staring after her wishing, hopelessly, that life was a little less complicated.

A few feet away from him young Gary coughed apologetically. Bognor had forgotten about him.

"I'm sorry, sir," he offered. "My orders are not to let anyone in without due authority. I didn't know you and the young lady were, like, acquainted."

Bognor smiled at him inanely. "That's quite all right, Gary," he said. "Quite all right. No harm done. Mrs. Bognor and I will be with you in just one moment. We thought we'd eat Rumanian tonight. Do you like Rumanian food?"

The Mountie frowned. "Can't say I know, Si, sir. But I guess Rumanians can grill a steak."

"I guess so too," said Bognor.

CHAPTER 12

Ainsley Cernik was surprisingly pleased at the idea of talking to Bognor. He was also, less surprisingly, tied up. However, hearing that the Bognors were leaving for home late that afternoon he did some swift rearranging of his schedule, and called back to say that if Bognor liked to come round to his squash club he could talk to him while he did a quick prelunch workout. Then perhaps their wives could join them for lunch. Bognor said that was fine, provided he could bring his personal bodyguard. Cernik asked if the bodyguard played squash. Bognor said he would find out and get him to bring a racket if he did.

Cernik's club was not remotely like Colonel Crombie's nor like such London sporting establishments as the Hurlingham or Queen's where, in trimmer days, Bognor had attempted to postpone the coming coronary by flailing around on the squash court. Cernik's club was aglow with young men and women who looked as if they existed on carrot juice, skim milk, Jacuzzis and prebreakfast marathons. These tended to be staff, but even the members, mainly middle-aged executives, had a bushy-tailed bounce which was a startling departure from previous generations nurtured on the three-martini lunch consumed in the smoke-filled room.

Bognor found Cernik in the gymnasium doing pull-ups. He stopped long enough to shake hands and establish the fact that Gary did not play squash.

"Too bad," he said, taking to the floor and embarking on a series of press-ups. He had the beginnings of a paunch but his biceps were enormous. Up down, up down. Bognor was impressed.

"Don't mind me," instructed Cernik. "Just ask whatever it is you want to ask. Go ahead. Shoot."

Bognor decided to begin with the most difficult question. He was not sure whether he had the advantage of the other man, but it was unusual for him to conduct interviews in gymnasia and he felt the circumstances demanded an unorthodox approach.

"I'm told that your father-in-law was going to cut your wife out of his will, if you persisted in fighting him over company policy."

Up, down, up down. Cernik never faltered. "Affirmative," he said.

"Ah." Bognor waited but his subject was evidently not going to amplify the answer.

"Did this worry you?" he tried.

Cernik was faltering, but through bodily rather than mental fatigue.

"Negative," he said, executing one final "up," springing to his feet and grabbing a rope which had been hanging from a wall bar. He began skipping. Bounce, bounce, bounce. Flick, flick, flick. Bognor watched, mesmerized for a second.

"So you were prepared to go on fighting Sir Roderick even though it meant you'd no longer stand to inherit the major shareholding in Mammoncorp?"

"Affirmative," said Cernik, changing rhythm, from a jump to a hop. He was sweating rivers. Perspiration trickled down his face and stained under his arms, but he was not in the least breathless. His mouth, fleshy, arguably sadistic, certainly sensual, remained resolutely shut. He breathed through his nose with military precision. Bognor was finding the whole business unnerving. He did not like a moving target. Perhaps it would be better to adopt an even more aggressive posture.

"Did you kill Sir Roderick?" he tried, unable to think of anything more bald and hostile.

Ainsley Cernik flung down the rope and started on squats. Slowly down to full knees bend, slowly up to attention. Down and up. Down and up. He executed the manoeuvre three times before answering. Indeed he took so long over the response that Bognor was on the point of repeating himself when Cernik said, from a crouching position:

"Negative."

Obviously, reasoned Bognor, he would have to ask a question which could not be answered by "yes," "no" or equivalents thereof. It would have to be carefully phrased. After discarding a number of promising queries he tried: "Do you have any thoughts about who might have done it, and if so can you let me know what they are?" In terms of conventional interrogation techniques this would have been dismissed by solid professionals like Pete Smith as a "no-no." Cernik, however, gave a sharp snort of laughter.

"You and I are going to get along just fine," he said, breaking off from the squats and wiping his brow on the back of his arm. "Come along to the squash court. We can be a little more private there." There were only two others in the gym, both middle-aged, and they were energetically minding their own business. Nevertheless it was as well to be sure.

The squash court had a gallery, and Bognor, assisted by Gary, ascended its stairs and leaned against the parapet watching Cernik thump the ball relentlessly against the back wall. He had comparatively little style but he was strong and he had a good eye.

"Okay," he said, picking up the ball from a back corner, "Prideaux might have done it. The RCMP are convinced Prideaux did it because Prideaux is a Quebecois extremist." He hit the ball up, and started returning his own shot again and again, punctuating his spiel with litttle grunts every time he laid gut to rubber. "That doesn't convince me. My reading of Prideaux, for whom by the way, I have no respect whatsoever, is that he is a weak man with only a marginal dedication to his cause. Okay, he is what they call "a sleeper," well my reading is that he'll stay asleep. Besides, my father-in-law was too interested in number one to be as antifrog as people now say." He hit a cross-court drive into the back corner again, and went to retrieve it. "Amos could have done it. I guess he knew Farquhar was going to leave him the ranch and the horses. But I don't believe Amos would have killed for that. He was happy to hang in. He got on all right with the boss. Any road, he knew how ill he was. He was probably the only one of us who knew how sick the old buzzard really was." He killed the ball again, and glanced up at the gallery. "You reading me?" he enquired. "Can you hear me? Am I making sense?"

"Yes, thanks." The acoustics were not that good, especially when Cernik's voice was competing against the squash ball being hacked against the wall. Cernik glanced at his watch. "I'm going to knock it off," he said, suddenly, "I'll see you downstairs. We'll go on talking while I change."

Outside the court Cernik tapped his racket against Bognor's plaster. "Howdya do that?" he asked.

"Skiing," said Bognor.

"Not what I heard."

"Oh, and what did you hear?"

Cernik led the way through the gymnasium, where the population had increased quite dramatically. Hordes of middle-aged men were working out on bicycling machines, rowing machines, chest-expanding machines, stomach-contracting machines. Bognor had never seen so much perspiring flesh.

"I heard otherwise," said Cernik grinning. He eyed Bognor's paunch. "You like a membership here?" he enquired.

Bognor pulled a face. "I haven't played squash in years."

"You should. Do you good. I'll give you a complimentary membership before you leave. Get some of that flab off. Soon as you're off those crutches."

Bognor raised his eyebrows. "Can you do that? I mean, it's a club isn't it? Don't you have to be proposed and seconded? Can't you be blackballed?"

"It's only *called* a club." Cernik gazed round at the members. "Gives it a touch of class. It's a business. Very good business too."

They passed out of the gym and into a corridor, where they stopped in front of the lifts. Cernik pressed the call button. "And I own it," he said, grinning broadly.

The lift arrived. It was dark brown, leather-lined and empty. A machine played conveyor-belt, Bach-inspired Musak. Cernik pressed the topmost button, marked P. "Penthouse," he said.

"Yours too?"

"Bright guy. Right in one."

They ascended. For a moment Bognor was reminded of yesterday's excitement. This, however, was different, if only because you couldn't see out. Seeing was not only believing. It was being scared witless too.

"Nothing to do with Mammon?" he asked.

"Nope." Cernik grinned again. "Which is why, frankly, being cut out of daddy-in-law's inheritance would have been no very big deal. We can survive without it."

They came to a halt, the door slid open and they emerged into a palatial reception area. A fountain played in the centre amid a rockery of fronds and ferns. The walls were hung with quite good oils on Canadian autumnal themes. A blonde, heavily tanned, in a very low cut orange blouse sat behind a kidney-shaped desk with a computer keyboard in front of her and an impressively space-age telephone device.

"Hi, Mr. Cernik," she simpered. "Colonel Crombie called. Otherwise no one."

"That schmuck," said Cernik as they passed through electrically operated doors into a sixty-foot drawing room with a plate-glass window overlooking the city. They were at least half a mile farther inland than Bognor's hotel, but the view, if less watery, was just as spectacular. The CN Tower dominated right of centre.

"Do you think Colonel Crombie might have done it?"

"He would if he could. But he doesn't have the guts or the intelligence. I suppose he was the one who told you about Eleanor and the inheritance."

"I don't think I should say," said Bognor primly.

"Please yourself. He'd have got it from that old freak Dolores. Can you use a drink? I would hazard a guess that you're into alcohol. Nothing personal."

"Er," said Bognor, feeling put out, "I—"

"Scotch? Gin?" Cernik was already putting ice into a tall glass. Bognor settled for a gin and tonic. Gary said he didn't touch alcohol while on duty and Cernik poured him a Perrier and another for himself with half a dozen ice cubes and a slice of lime.

"Okay. This way, gentlemen," he said, and led the way through more electric doors to a bathroom area complete with Jacuzzi, sauna and all the other ablutionary extras favoured by the very rich. "Dolores could have done it," he said, stripping off to reveal a well-muscled body, hairy as a spider monkey's. "She's tough enough but I have a hunch she was still a little in love with the old boy, despite all that happened. And he was looking after her very well. She had cause to be grateful." He picked up a familiar bottle from a marble slab and waved it under Bognor's nose. "The famous murder weapon, eh?" he laughed. "Monsieur's personal bath oil. Only time he ever smelled like roses." He chuckled, and sloshed a couple of shakes into the bubbling Jacuzzi.

"What the hell?" he said, easing into the water. "You have one of these things? Kinda sexy, eh?" Bognor confessed that he had no Jacuzzi.

"Pity. Would you mind passing my drink?"

Gary handed Cernik his Perrier water, and the little tycoon stood in his whirlpool drinking it, sweat still beading his brow. "I'll bet one thing, though," he said, when he had satisfied the most immediate demands of his thirst, "I'll bet Crombie never mentioned his own motive."

"His own motive?" Bognor would have liked Crombie to be a serious suspect.

"I thought not," said Cernik, bending down so that only his head was not covered in water. "He didn't tell you about the wedding plans. 'La la la-la.'" He hummed the opening bars of the Mendelssohn march and stared at Bognor enquiringly.

"No," said Bognor. "You mean him and Dolores. Him and La Bandanna."

"Right again. Bright kid."

"But what has that got to do with it?" Bognor's gin was so frozen it almost stuck to his lips. They felt numb. His brain was proceeding in a similar direction.

Cernik heaved himself out of the pool and began to dry himself vigorously on a dark-chocolate towel of enormous proportions. "I won't ask you gentlemen to step into the sauna. Fact is, I'll cut out the sauna today." He wrapped the towel togalike about him and motioned them to follow. This time they found themselves in a dressing room. More brown leather. Cernik went to a long wall cupboard and selected one from a choice of about a dozen apparently identical blazers, one from a choice of about thirty pairs of light-grey flannel slacks, and then bent over to choose one from the file of snazzy Gucci-style black sneakers. To this he added a white shirt and a navy-and-magenta striped tie in the style of the Guards Brigade, only vulgar with it.

"So maybe Crombie and Dolores did do the wicked deed, eh?" Cernik abandoned the towel briefly and stood naked on the antique reproduction scales where he adjusted a weight or two before stepping off with a smug expression. "One fifty-three," he said. "Haven't been over one fifty-six since I came here in sixty-eight."

"I still don't understand," pleaded Bognor, despairingly. "Why should Colonel Crombie and Dolores Crump kill Sir Roderick Farquhar because they wanted to get married?"

"Negative dowry situation." Cernik buttoned up his shirt and got to work on the tie, knotting it in fluid flamboyant gestures. He managed to ooze a treacle of self-confidence even when he was dressing. Bognor was impressed yet repelled. He was always nervous in the presence of power, still more in the presence of what some people called "animal magnetism." Cernik, he decided, was an animal magnet.

"What is a negative dowry situation?" he asked.

Cernik pulled on the slacks and tucked his shirt inside, pulled in his stomach and looked momentarily disappointed.

"A dowry situation," he spoke slowly and patiently, as if to a backward child, "means that on marriage the bride's father gives the groom some goats or cattle or maybe money. You know, like to soften the blow. I even had some shekels when I took Eleanor off the old man's hands. Old established custom. Right?"

"Right."

"So a negative dowry situation is what Dolores was into. Farquhar made her a hefty allowance, the house in Saratoga, the Manhattan apartment. You know the deal. The condition was that she didn't hitch herself to anyone else, least of all Crombie."

"So Dolores and the colonel wanted to get married and Farquhar told them he'd turn her out of the houses and cut off her pension?"

Cernik preened himself in front of the mirror, found a handkerchief from a chest of drawers, stuffed it in his breast pocket, arranged it carefully, sprayed himself with aftershave or "splashon," and combed his hair, thus concealing the incipient bald spot at the back which Bognor was delighted to notice. Then he said, "Right on, dummy. If the old flapper spliced with the colonel she stood to lose a million dollars in property—maybe more—plus an annuity of a hundred thousand a year, inflation-linked. That ain't chicken feed. Especially where Dolores is concerned. No way she's going to make a living out of her one traditional asset. That's gone. Crombie is her last chance. If she doesn't drag the colonel to the altar it's little-old-ladies-ville for La Bandanna. She used to be some looker, I tell you. And she could turn it on. But not anymore. Comes a time when all of us have to hang up our ballet shoes, eh?" He gave one final pat to the top of his head. "Let's go eat," he said. Bognor wondered how long it would be before he was into hair transplants.

The dining room was panelled in mahogany and hung with Krieghoffs. The table was mahogany, the silver was silver, the crystal, crystal. The water was water, the lettuce, cucumber, diced carrot, cottage cheese, crisp bread and other wondrously healthy, calorie-free, nutritious comestibles were equally undeceptive.

They were, to Bognor's horror, no more and no less than what they seemed. Monica, who had had an appointment at the hairdresser's, had evidently been chatting to Eleanor Cernik for some time. The Bognors exchanged surreptitious glances of mutual commiseration. Eleanor Cernik, dressed though she was in the most expensive little two-piece Dior could conjure up, adorned too with rings and a brooch of emerald and diamond, was still surprisingly mousey. Perhaps a life sandwiched between two aggressive animal magnets like Cernik and Farquhar had given her no alternative, but Bognor had met many wives and mistresses of rich and famous men who were formidable harridans in their own right. Eleanor, however, was not in this class. She was not given to self-assertion.

"Ainsley and I used to eat meat," she said, a little timidly, "but we gave it up the same time I stopped smoking. I used to smoke twenty a day, would you believe?"

"I expect you feel a lot better for it," said Bognor jocosely.

"I guess so," she said thoughtfully. "I know I'd feel a whole lot worse if I was still smoking."

Inwardly Bognor sighed. Outwardly he smiled politely.

After a while Cernik, who had been making small talk to Monica, drew the conversation back under his control.

"Mr. Bognor wanted to know whether we killed your father," he called across the mahogany. "Crombie told him about him threatening to cut you out."

"Oh, that!" said Eleanor, crunching carrot.

Bognor waited for amplification, but none was forthcoming.

"I wonder if we'll ever know for certain." Cernik cracked a piece of crisp bread and flashed a wide smile at Monica. "Looks to me like the perfect crime. Whatever which way you attack, you have to concede that there are a hundred and one motives. Even we had a reason to kill him." There was the beginning of a protest from his wife, but he talked through it. "Now that is not the same as saying that we did it, but Eleanor and I can prove nothing. We had some of that damn bath oil. Still have, as I showed you. Like the others we have the money and the connections to arrange the chemical substitution necessary. That's not a problem. We all of us had enough access to the old man's million and one bathrooms around the place, to slip the deadly bottle into position. So I simply do not see how in hell you are going to hang this on anyone, without the murderer cracking up."

"Which is perfectly possible." Bognor did not believe this, on present form, but he felt he should say it.

Cernik demurred. "You're dealing with some tough numbers here, Mr. Bognor. I don't see any of them cracking. But I sure as hell wish they would. The uncertainty is doing no good to anyone, least of all the Mammon Corporation."

"It all seems so . . . oh, so unnecessary." Eleanor spoke with a vehemence Bognor had not been expecting as she pushed her half-finished cheese and vegetables to one side. "If only they could have waited."

"I'm sorry . . ." Bognor helped down some cottage cheese with a gulp of water, and waited for amplification.

"He'd have been dead in two weeks. A month at most. There was no *need*. No *need* at all."

Bognor turned to their host, eyebrow cocked in a mute question mark.

Cernik nodded. "Affirmative," he agreed, laconically. "We talked with the specialists in London. They'd tried everything. There was nothing left, so they stitched him up and sent him home to die. He was in a terminal cancer situation."

"Did he know?"

"Oh, yeah." Cernik shoved the last of his lettuce into his mouth, chewed reflectively and put down his knife and fork. "Oh, yeah," he repeated. "He knew."

CHAPTER 13

They did not enjoy flying. The plane was too big. There were too many passengers. For some reason they were diverted through Montreal's cavernous white elephant of an airport at Mirabelle, which put an extra hour on the flight. There was a blizzard and Bognor was convinced that it was unsafe to attempt takeoff. The film was an adaptation of a Neil Simon play which Bognor had seen already. He would have preferred *The Mousetrap*. He had abandoned his crutches, but his leg was still stiff and emplastered. When he stuck it into the aisle people kept tripping over it on the way to the loo until a stewardess had to come and complain. The food was almost as bad as their lunch and though there was alleged to be meat in the main course he was certain it was spun protein. He bought a headset to listen to music but the rubber bits that fitted into his ears fell off and the plastic prongs gave him earache. He bought a Dick Francis at the airport and discovered after they were airborne that he had read it already. He tried sleep but it eluded him. By his side Monica, who always travelled with special flying slippers and a face mask, lay back, out cold, mouth open, snoring lightly. Bognor fumed.

To while away the time he made lists of suspects and motives and opportunities. He wrote thumbnail sketches of all those he had interviewed. He tried to think himself into the position of Sir Roderick himself, a rich, malevolent old man with a sentence of death passed on him. Would he, perhaps, try suicide? He guessed not, though he could not be sure. His impression was that a man like Farquhar would hang on to the bitter end, half believing in his immortality and half believing that a miracle might happen. But if not . . . And who was trying to frighten Bognor away? Succeeding, moreover, he acknowledged ruefully.

After all if it had not been for the telephone calls and that unpleasant experience on the CN Tower he and Monica would still
be in Canada. Not perhaps getting anywhere, but doing their
best. They had not seen Niagara Falls. He had not given La Bandanna Rose a touch of the third degree. It had been, he was
forced to concede, a flop and he had the scars to prove it. That
untouchable imbecile Baker. Would he be Canada's next prime
minister? Beyond belief. But they had had some rum premiers in
the past. For such a conventional country to have chosen Mac-
kenzie King—or Trudeau, come to that. But the idea of Baker was
preposterous. A PM who threw bottles of Chivas at his wife's
presumed lovers. Inconceivable. Bognor ordered a split of champagne from a passing hostess, a dark, skinny girl with big black
kohl-rimmed eyes. He thought wistfully of Louise and drank her
an apologetic little toast in champagne. Nice girl. Pretty girl.
He glanced across at Monica's open mouth and toyed with the
idea of pouring a drop of champagne into it. No. A waste. She
would only choke on it. On the other side of the plane a small
child lifted the window blind to reveal some rosy-fingered dawn.
He consulted his watch. They must be over Ireland by now.

He must have drifted off in the end because he woke to find
them beginning the descent to Heathrow. Monica was finishing
breakfast. She looked fresh as a mountain stream.

"Sleep well?" she asked. "I didn't wake you for breakfast. You
looked so sweet all sprawled out. Like a teddy bear."

Bognor growled. He had been dreaming. A confused dream in
which he had been forced to drink buckets of bath oil by a squad
of lumberjacks and Mounties. "Who do you think did it?" he
asked, as the no-smoking signs came on and the engines changed
pitch, inducing fear and uncertainty in Bognor's suggestible imagination.

"Funny," said Monica, handing her tray to the harassed girl
with the big black eyes, "I was just wondering that."

"And?"

"I think he did it himself."

"No suicide note? No warning? No explanation?"

Monica pondered. "I know it's not usual but it is possible. He obviously wasn't terribly close to anyone in particular. And he was also, to put it mildly misanthopic. Misanthropes leave no letters."

"No?"

"No," she said, decidedly. Below them London appeared through the clouds. They could see the Thames snaking sullenly across the city like a grey tapeworm.

"Looks awfully drab down there," he said, gloomily.

"Not as cold as Toronto."

"Damp though. And not such good central heating."

"Not as dangerous."

"Don't you believe it. Just as much chance of being hit on the head in London as there is in Toronto. I speak from experience."

Monica smiled.

"You still make me laugh," she said, "even after all these years. Even *more* after all these years."

"Huh." Bognor was not sure about this. He knew the laughter was affectionate, but it was laughter nonetheless. Being laughed at was all very well in its way, but not virile. He bet no one laughed at Ainsley Cernik. He put a hand in his pocket and fingered his life membership of the Macdonald-Cartier Squash Club. He didn't suppose he'd ever use it even if he ever went back, which he doubted.

"Bath oil?" he mused. "It's an odd way to commit suicide. Why go to all that trouble? Why not an overdose? Or if he wanted to do it in the bath, why not slit his wrists?"

"Maybe he wanted to set some final conundrum," said Monica. "It's one way to be remembered."

"Not that anyone's likely to forget him in a hurry." The undercarriage went down with a rasping crash that set Bognor's nerves jangling.

"It does seem odd," he went on, "that he should have given out bath oil as Christmas presents and then used the same bath oil to kill himself."

"Hang on." Monica pulled her seat belt tight. "You're jumping a lot of guns."

"No, but," Bognor persisted, "if he did kill himself then it is rather peculiar that he should have sent out the bottles as Christmas presents. What could it mean?"

Monica thought for a moment. "Put it slightly differently," she said. "If he really wanted to set a conundrum what better way to do it than hand out the bottles and then use a bottle to kill himself. I mean, suppose you want to spread a little confusion. Right. First of all you hand out a quantity of rather rare sawn-off shotguns to people you wish to be suspected of a murder. Then you shoot yourself with a sawn-off shotgun of the same make or calibre or whatever the distinguishing features of shotguns are. And, hey presto, all the people to whom you gave shotguns become suspects."

"But," said Bognor, eagerly, "there's a flaw in that. It would obviously be suicide because they'd find *your* own shotgun by your corpse."

"Yes, but with bath oil that doesn't matter."

The plane touched down with a heavy double bump. The engine raced. Mr. and Mrs. Bognor gripped each other's hands tightly.

Most of that day they slept, rising only in time to go out to dinner. They had a curry, a particular treat since Indian restaurants, unlike Chinese, appeared to be in short supply in southern Ontario. Next morning, quite bright and early, Bognor reported back to work at the Board of Trade. He was walking quite nimbly now, and his rib cage was giving much less pain. His face too was almost mended. Even so, as he tottered along the peeling corridors of power and influence he attracted gratifying remarks of commiseration and concern. When he reported to Parkinson he was not in the least surprised, however, to find that his boss's greeting was rather more peremptory. Parkinson was bored, even mildly disgusted, by illness and injury, in others. It was an indication of failure, not a badge of courage.

"Aha, Bognor," he said not even looking up, but pretending to be engrossed in whatever it was that he was writing in fussy strokes with a blue felt-tipped pen. "Close the door. There's an energy crisis. We have to conserve heat." Bognor kicked it shut with his better leg. Parkinson looked up shortly, said nothing, looked volumes, and returned to his scribbling. "Sit down, sit down," he said, "I'll be with you in a moment."

Bognor sat and stared at the portrait of Her Majesty. It was always deflating to come home.

"Good," said Parkinson at last, flinging down the pen and appraising his subordinate with an unflinching gaze. "Well, well. We have been in the wars."

"Yes, we have rather."

"Tsk, tsk. Sorry about that. You know I prefer members of the department to be resolute in maintaining the low profile."

"Yes, I know. I *am* sorry."

"I'm sure. Hurt, does it?"

"Not so bad now. One gets used to it. It was painful at the time."

"They talked about brain damage." Parkinson allowed the remark to hang in the air, half question, half statement, so that Bognor waited before replying.

"No brain damage."

Parkinson beamed soullessly. "Excellent. No brain damage. And the leg. You'll regain full use of that in due course, I've no doubt."

"I believe so, yes." Bognor smiled sardonically. "They're not even going to amputate."

"Good, good." Parkinson rubbed his hands together and beamed again. "So no harm done, eh?"

"I suppose not."

"And what do you have to report?"

"Report?"

"Report, yes. R-E-P-O-R-T. Report. Have you solved the insoluble? Is the murderer incarcerated and awaiting trial? Or were you merely rushing in where angels fear to tread?"

"Frankly I'm beginning to wonder if it was murder actually."

"I see." Parkinson put his fingers together and stared morosely along the top of them, as if lining his minion up for summary execution.

"Not a murder actually." Parkinson appeared to brood on this. "Life in the old corpse yet. Is that it? Sir Roderick Farquhar not dead but frozen alive. Is that what you had in mind?"

"I had a thought about suicide."

"A thought about suicide." Parkinson nodded several times. "Good, good. Excellent. Well, I know, Bognor, that, as usual, I can rely upon you to keep your thoughts to yourself."

Bognor opened his mouth, thought better of it, and shut it again.

"That's an order, Bognor. Meanwhile you will naturally furnish me with your written report in triplicate by nine hundred hours tomorrow morning. Oh, and you'll be glad to hear that I had a wire from RCMP HQ informing me that you had been safely escorted off the premises and the matter was now back under control. They expect to be arresting some Frenchman as soon as the political situation allows it. I gather they've been having trouble with Ottawa. They should come over here and see what I have to contend with at Westminster. Out of the mouths of babes and . . . Oh, well, some of these so-called Ministers are scarcely out of nappies, but that's my problem, not yours, thank God."

He stood up, the gesture inviting Bognor to do the same.

"Good to have you back," he said. "Now, if you'll excuse me, I have work to do. You cut along and write that report and then we'll find some appropriate light duties to keep you out of further mischief. We're woefully behind on positive vetting. I think we'll give you a couple of weeks of that to see you right again and get you back in the swing."

Bognor swore under his breath. "Right you are," he said. "Good to be back." He hoped, as he limped defiantly down the passage, that the irony shone through.

The report was a bore. He disliked writing them and he was enough of a realist to appreciate that this particular one would be little more than a catalogue of failure. At least it was a failure at this point. There was one further interview which might just change that, and before he even started to marshal his thoughts, he telephoned Farquhar's London doctor and managed to make an appointment for just after lunch.

The doctor's rooms in Harley Street turned out to be opulent and distinguished in a way that Harrison Bentley would have adored but could never emulate. The furniture had been accumulated over a long period of time, rather than bought in a job lot from Harrods. The nineteenth-century watercolours were a particular hobby of the doctor's. The library of medical books though quite precious first editions were regularly consulted. The only magazines were *Country Life, The Connoisseur* and *Apollo.* The doctor himself was elegant, silver-haired, sixtyish, a stylish real tennis player, a member of the MCC and Pratt's. His charges were what one would expect. His clientele, increasingly, tended to come from the Middle East, a circumstance which distressed him, but not inordinately.

"I've had to squeeze you in, I'm afraid." He spoke in a soft, almost sibilant manner which managed at one and the same time to be immensely deferential and extraordinarily condescending. "There does seem to be a lot of illness about. Mustn't complain. But you haven't come to discuss your symptoms unless I'm much mistaken." He put his head on one side and half smiled an invitation to impart a confidence. At a certain level, Bognor considered, doctors find it impossible to abandon the bedside manner.

"I've come about one of your patients."

"Ye-e-es." He smiled, encouraging Bognor to continue.

"It's rather a long shot. I wanted to know whether or not this patient is or rather was intending to commit suicide."

The doctor coughed. "You must understand, Mr. Bognor, that the medical profession is bound by a code of ethics. There is an oath. It would be most improper to discuss one of my patients with a third party. Unless they were family and then only in exceptional circumstances. You're not family, I take it?"

"No." Bognor had the impression that the doctor was playing games with him. "No, I'm not family. I'm Board of Trade."

"Quite." The doctor waited.

"The fact is," said Bognor, "that your patient is a late patient. That is to say he died."

"That would naturally put a different complexion on the matter."

"You could talk about a dead patient?"

"Under certain circumstances." The doctor looked up at the

grandmother clock which ticked sonorously in a corner of the room. "I'm sorry, Mr. Bognor, but I don't have very much time. You've come to talk about the late Sir Roderick Farquhar."

Bognor nodded. "But how did you know?"

"Let's just leave that for now. Am I to understand that you are involved in a murder investigation?"

"Yes."

"And has anyone been charged?"

"No."

"Oh." He looked quite crestfallen. "Then I'm sorry. I don't think I can be of help."

"What do you mean?" Bognor was flabbergasted.

"I can't help you unless someone has been charged with Sir Roderick's murder." The doctor's mouth set tight. His charm seemed in the balance.

"But I can't charge anyone unless you help me," Bognor pleaded.

"Then we're caught in a vicious circle."

"But that's ridiculous!" Bognor could not believe what he was hearing. "Let's get it absolutely straight. If I come back and say that someone has been charged with Sir Roderick's murder then you will help me. Otherwise not?"

"That's exactly it." The doctor smiled, more friendly now. "Look," he said, "I'm not being wilfully obstructive, I'm really not. Shortly before he died—the last time I saw him—Sir Roderick gave me a letter. It was addressed to you." Bognor's jaw sagged. "It was not to be given to you until after his death," he waved aside Bognor's attempted interruption, "and not only after his death. After someone had been accused of murdering him."

"You mean he knew he was going to be murdered?"

"That I can't say."

"Can you tell me how ill he was?"

Again the doctor appeared to think for a moment, then he replied: "Very ill. It was a cancer of course. There were complications. I personally gave him about a fortnight to a month, but you can never tell in these cases. He might have dropped dead the second he got outside the door. Or he might have struggled on for, oh, three months. Even more."

"And in the end?"

"He died about three weeks after leaving these rooms." The doctor paused dramatically. "But not, as you are aware, of cancer."

"I see." Bognor's usual cover for hopeless confusion. He sighed. "But I can't have this letter unless someone has been charged with his murder?"

"Precisely."

"Okay," said Bognor, gloomily. "I'll have to see what I can do. I'll be back."

The doctor smiled. "I admire your optimism," he said.

It took Bognor three quarters of an hour to return by taxi to the Board of Trade, and it was almost four o'clock before he was finally seated in his own grubby cubbyhole in the bowels of the building, surrounded by central heating pipes, faded notices, chipped teacups and unanswered mail. That meant it was midmorning in Toronto. He asked the operator to get him a personal call to Pete Smith and waited in a state of high excitement, the first time he had been in such a state while waiting to talk to Smith, and probably the last. Eventually, after three false starts he was through to the right Smith in the right town in the right country.

"Hi, Si." The ponderous voice came thudding across the Atlantic. "Great to hear you. How're things?"

"Fine thanks. And you?"

"Minus eight degrees Celsius in Metro, Si. Snowing hard. And the Leafs were shut out by the Kings last night."

"In LA or at the Gardens?"

"At the Gardens, would you believe."

"Gosh, Pete, that's terrible."

"Sure is, Si. Mrs. Bognor okay? She recover from that upset on the CN Tower?"

"Yes thanks. I say, Pete. There's something I think you ought to know. You might be able to help. I don't know. It's about the Farquhar murder."

A distinct pause. Bognor thought he had done enough ingratiating to soften him up. Evidently not. "Yeah, Si?" Definitely suspicious.

"I went to see old Farquhar's doctor today. He told me that Farquhar was definitely terminally ill. He only had a few days left."

The Mountie whistled. "Is that right, eh? Someone went to a lot of trouble for nothing."

"It does look like it," said Bognor. "But the most extraordinary thing is that Farquhar left me a letter."

"Is that a fact? And what did it say?"

"I haven't read it. I don't know."

"Haven't read it? Jeez, Si, that could be an important letter."

"I am aware of that," said Bognor tetchily. "It's not for the want of trying. I haven't been able to read it because I haven't been given it."

Long pause. Then, "Say again, Si."

"It *is* eccentric," Bognor admitted. "Sir Roderick left the letter with his doctor here in London, the one I told you about, and his instructions were that I was not to be given it unless someone was charged with Sir Roderick's murder."

"This is a very bad line, Si. Would it help if I called you back?"

"There's nothing wrong with the line, Pete. It's the idea that's difficult to get hold of. My theory is that this is Sir Roderick Farquhar's suicide letter."

"Suicide letter?"

"That's my theory."

"Say, Si, you're way ahead of me on this one. Now you say you can't have this letter unless we arrest someone?"

"Yes."

"Doesn't matter who?"

"No."

"I'll have to talk to Ottawa, Si. This sure is dynamite. Maybe they'll let me bring in that French bastard and charge him."

"He'd do," said Bognor. "But my point is that anyone will do. You can charge *Gary* if you want, it doesn't matter. You just have to be able to say to this doctor chappie that you have arrested someone for the murder of Sir Roderick Farquhar. Okay?"

"I read you, Si. I'll do what I can. I'd sure as hell like to know what Farquhar put in that letter."

"Good," said Bognor. "Let's talk tomorrow."

That night he sat up late working on the report. It was heavy going. Monica made him a series of Buck Rarebits and when he had finished those he moved on to slim cigars and whisky toddies. Chain smoking and chain drinking. Not good for the figure or the complexion but essential for report writing. The problem was imposing order on chaos, convincing Parkinson that he had proceeded in the methodical, frankly boring manner prescribed by the Board of Trade's Special Operations Department's ground rules, operatives for the use of. He had, of course, done nothing of the sort. Never did. Whenever he tried, something came up. Like strange ladies giving him tickets to execrable performances of *The Mousetrap* or strange gentlemen pursuing him across the snow-swept wastes of the Toronto Metro Zoo. Proceeding according to the book yielded no pleasure and no result. Flying by the ample seat of his baggy pants was altogether to be preferred. Gut feeling was what counted. The problem was convincing Parkinson. In this case, what was so tiresome was that the solution was about to be made known, in the shape of the dead man's last letter, and yet Parkinson had insisted on having the report on his desk, in triplicate, by first thing next morning. Well, he would miss the deadline. Or at the very least leave room for a long postscript.

"What was it you said?" he asked his wife as he came to bed, thoughtlessly waking her as he sat, inadvertently, on one of her feet, which had strayed over to his side of the nuptial couch. "Misanthropes leave no letters?"

"Probably," said Monica. "It sounds like me. Was he a complete misanthrope?"

"He liked ladies," said Bognor. "Sexually that is."

"Hate your neighbour, love your neighbour's wife."

"That's right. Is that you too?"

Monica sat up. "Are you coming to bed or not?" she asked impatiently. "It's a paraphrase of Macaulay. Macaulay's description of Byron's ethics, if you must know."

"So Farquhar was a latter-day Byron?"

"Macaulay would say he was a disciple. Perhaps. Anyway, I was wrong."

"Wrong?"

"He did leave a letter."

Bognor undressed and put on his pyjamas. He still found such manoevres difficult and marginally painful, but not as much as he liked to pretend.

"Oh," he moaned, glumly, as he pulled the quilt up to his chin and listened to his wife's regular, fast-asleep breathing. "If only . . ."

CHAPTER 14

Next morning he had a mild hangover which he quickly set to rights with a couple of Alka-Seltzer and a plate of bacon and egg. For some reason he was feeling aggressive and ebullient. Today was the day. Today all would be revealed. He whistled on his way to work, hummed *Aïda* in the tube, provoking curious and hostile glances. At the office, summoned by Parkinson, he was positively breezy about the not quite finished report.

"Won't be a tick now," he told Parkinson.

Parkinson looked sour. "I asked you to have it done by this morning."

"It is. Almost. But not in triplicate. It's not typed up yet. And there are just a few finishing touches. An 'i' here, a 't' there. Dottings and crossings. Verstehen Sie?"

"You feeling all right, Bognor?"

"Not too bad actually."

"Leg working again okay?"

"Yes. Rose up and walked."

"I'd prefer it if you did not blaspheme in this office," said Parkinson grimly. "I worry about you, Bognor, I really do. How is it that you came to be in this department?"

"We've been through that a thousand and one times," Bognor grinned. "Administrative error."

Parkinson shook his head several times and drummed his pencil on the desk top.

"Should have had you transferred years ago," he said.

"Aha. But you didn't. Because secretly, you like having me around the place, as well you know."

Parkinson said nothing but contemplated his subordinate with ruminative distaste. Then he picked a brown folder from his "pending" tray.

"Here's your positive vetting subject," he said. "Some sociology wallah from the University of Sussex being posted to the Cabinet Office. Usual drill. And do please remember that sociology is not a crime."

"I know, I know." Bognor grinned again. "A sin not a crime. A matter of morality not an indictable offence."

"Oh, get out," shouted Parkinson. "You're insufferable this morning. And don't come back till you're servile and depressed again."

Bognor knew when he was in danger of overstepping the mark. He turned and limped out, not allowing himself another word.

He phoned Toronto immediately after a disgusting canteen lunch. It was 9 A.M. their time.

"Hi, Si. Good to hear you. We nailed him."

"You did? That's terrific. Wonderful news." Bognor's heart leaped. There was no need today for an exchange of temperatures or hockey scores. This was a meeting of minds, two ace investigators working in concert.

"Ottawa's scared," said Smith. "Federal-Provincial Relations are up in arms. All the frog ministers in cabinet complaining. It's hell up there."

"How did you pull it off?"

"Don't rightly know, Si. Our liaison guys lobbied Justice and Trade. In the end I figure the Mammoncorp share drop is what decided them. Besides Quebec's kind of quiet right now while they wait for the next referendum."

"And has he said anything?"

"We're letting him cool his heels for a while, Si. No reason to ask him too much till you've found out what's in that letter. If you're correct and that is a suicide note, then we just have to let the bastard go."

"Yes. I see that. Listen, Pete, what I'm going to do is this." He enunciated very carefully, willing himself to remember that he was dealing with a foreigner of below average IQ, and one who, in the past at least, had not concealed his misgivings about Bognor's patronizing British ways. "I am going straight round to Harley Street to where this doctor lives and I am going to telephone from there. When I have spoken to you I am going to hand you over to the doctor and you will identify yourself and confirm to him that you have arrested Jean-Claude Prideaux and charged him with the murder of Sir Roderick Farquhar. Is that clear?"

"Clear as a bell, Si baby." Goodness, thought Bognor, he is mellowing.

He put the receiver down, then phoned through to Farquhar's doctor and arranged to come round at once. He thought of referring to Parkinson but remembered his boss's sour expression that morning and decided against. This was his own coup. He would present it to Parkinson when it was a fait accompli and he could claim the credit, the whole credit and nothing but the credit.

At Harley Street he was shown straight into the doctor's presence. He, suave and dapper, as the day before, affected to express surprise.

"Quick work, Mr. Bognor, though I must say it hardly inspires confidence in the forces of international law and order. It is usually so easy to charge people with murder?"

"The Mounties have been wanting to arrest this man for weeks. It's only the international political situation which had been holding them back." Bognor spoke with an air of considerable self-importance.

"Ah," the doctor smiled knowingly, as if such considerations were his daily bread. "The only question now is proving that the charge has been made. Can you do that?"

"What I propose, sir"—Bognor tended towards the deferential when on a supposedly winning streak—"is that you should call International Enquiries and ask for the RCMP number in Toronto. That way you will know for certain that the number is correct. When you get through to the Mounties you ask to speak to Peter Smith. Smith is the man in charge of the Farquhar murder. He will confirm to you that he has made the charge."

The doctor appeared to think for a moment. "That sounds fair," he said eventually. "May I ask, by the way, against whom the charge has been made?"

"Chap called Prideaux. He was Sir Roderick's secretary."

"Ah yes, Prideaux." Another of those glacial introspective smiles. "I remember him well. Very well, then, let us proceed."

And so they proceeded. It went entirely according to plan. Directory Enquiries were able to find the number in less than five minutes and the International Exchange obtained it in less than ten. Smith did not muff his lines. The doctor was convinced.

"The letter is in my safe downstairs," he said to Bognor, "and your friend in Toronto would like a word. I'll go and fetch it while you talk to him."

Bognor took the receiver. "Well done, Pete. Just the ticket. How's Prideaux?"

"Mad as hell. He wants a lawyer. He's not saying nothing. Say, Si, there's something I didn't tell you."

"What now?" Bognor was not much interested in anything that Smith had to tell him now. All his attention was focussed on the posthumous words of Sir Roderick Farquhar, words addressed to him alone. It was an awesome moment.

"Our people arrested that French bastard at some cottage on Ward's Island."

"Oh, yes, I know it," said Bognor conversationally, then wished he hadn't.

"How come, Si?" The Mountie's voice had turned suspicious again. Bognor swore to himself. He must remember that their mutual goodwill was wafer-thin.

"Prideaux mentioned it," he said. "That's all. But what about it?"

"He was with a woman, Si," said Smith portentously. Bognor experienced a sudden onset of depression. Louise. He had assumed that the relationship between Prideaux and Louise was entirely political. This sounded sexual and it made him sad. "Our boys believe he was keeping this woman at the cottage against her will," continued Smith. "She had cuts and bruises consistent with being hit about by some bastard, and they think she may have been tied up." Bognor's emotions changed gear again. Now he was shocked, outraged, distressed. "French bastard" was not nearly strong enough. He recalled Louise's tearful, drawn appearance the last time he had seen her. How could he have done such a thing? "She was emotionally disturbed," said Smith. "Very emotionally disturbed. And she was keen to talk to you. Matter of fact, she said she had a very important story to tell but that you were the only person in the world to whom she was going to tell it. You must have made some impression on the lady, Si." Bognor experienced elation, joy, a renewed belief in himself and the essential goodness of life. "Only thing is, Si, I have to warn you that lady is dynamite, like she is bad news. She is one hundred per cent dangerous."

Bognor knit his brows in an expression of puzzlement. "Dangerous?" Pretty, intelligent, sad, vulnerable but surely not dangerous. "Are we talking about the same person, Pete?" he asked.

"I wouldn't know, Si." Now Smith sounded really self-important. "The lady I am talking about is Maggie Fox, wife of the Honourable John C. Baker."

"Oh," said Bognor. "Oh. I see." He closed his eyes and passed a hand across his forehead. It came away damp, though he was not certain why. He felt muddled and nervous.

"Anything wrong?" The doctor had come back into the room without his noticing. In his hand he held a stiff white envelope which he now gave to Bognor. On the outside in firm, looped, forward-sloping black-ink handwriting were the words, "Personal. Mr. Simon Bognor. Special Operations Department. Board of Trade, London, England." Bognor shook his head at the doctor, "No," he said, "I'm fine, thanks. Just a slight wrinkle in the arrangements on the other side of the Atlantic. Nothing too serious." Then speaking into the mouthpiece he said, "Hey, Pete, I am going to put the phone down for a second while I open the letter. Then I'll come right back."

There was a grunt of agreement from Smith and Bognor put the phone down and tore the envelope open with shaking fingers. There were several sheets of paper inside covered in the same black hand. Although it was large writing and there were not that many words to a page it was still a long letter.

"Dear Mr. Bognor,

"It may be that you will never have occasion to open this letter, but if your past performance and reputation are anything to go by I guess that you will become involved in the investigation which will surely follow my somewhat mysterious death. And I feel certain that only your peculiar brand of perverted logic and insane intuition will actually lead to anyone being accused of my murder. I have, as you may have surmised, no great love for my fellow men but at life's end I am allowing myself a final act of charity. No man shall be convicted for a murder which I myself committed. This letter is to explain to you that my death is not murder but suicide. I have killed myself."

Bognor exhaled a long, drawn out, conclusive sigh which signified the end of the road. There had been a deal of needless hustle and bustle to arrive at this moment. He had the scars to prove it. It was not in his heart to forgive the dead man, and yet there was something chillingly pathetic in this message from beyond the grave. He put it to one side and returned to the transatlantic telephone.

"Pete," he said, in a voice grave to a point not far short of sepulchral, "it's as I thought."

"Oh, yeah?"

"There's no doubt about it. It's a suicide note. You'll have to let Prideaux go. And there had better be a formal announcement. Hang on, I'll read you the relevant passage." He picked up the letter and repeated the crucial words: "No man shall be convicted for a murder which I myself committed. This letter is to explain to you that my death is not murder but suicide. I have killed myself!"

There was a delay before Smith's reply and his voice when it came was laden with frustration and disappointment. "Guess that's kind of conclusive Si," he conceded. "That Prideaux guy will have to go free, goddammit. You sure that's Farquhar's handwriting. It really is his letter?" Bognor glanced at the doctor. "It's his, is it?" he asked. "Authentic Farquhar?" The doctor nodded. "Affirmative," said Bognor, "to quote the deceased's unloved son-in-law. It's a long letter. I won't read it now. I suppose I'd better bring it over with me. You'll have to have it and there's no way I am going to entrust it to Her Majesty's mails."

"Right on, Si." There was no mistaking the gloom in the Mountie's voice. "Just let me know your flight and I'll have a limo meet you at the airport. I'm kinda sorry it turned out like this. But thanks for your help. It's not your fault."

"I agree." Bognor, too, felt oddly let down, though he couldn't explain quite why. After all, they had their solution. He and Pete Smith said their good-byes, then Bognor gathered up the letter and thrust it into his disintegrating brown leather briefcase, and was shown out into the street. He took a cab back home. His report could perfectly well be composed at home. Parkinson should be pleased. In the end, by luck rather than judgement perhaps, Bognor had as usual, got his man. The man was dead, true, but a line could be drawn under the report and "finis" could be written. A ribbon could be tied about it and it could be consigned to the files, there to await an eager researcher in the years to come. Bognor ought to have been pleased.

He did not read the rest of the letter until he got home. Monica had been helping out at her friend Sara Blackrock's art gallery, one of the many part-time occupations in which she indulged from time to time. She had stopped off at the delicatessen for various frozen gourmet dinner items. Bognor himself had stopped off at the off-licence for a bottle of Cliquot and another of Marques de Riscal. They would help to alleviate his sense of anticlimax.

"Are you sitting comfortably?" he asked Monica when he had opened the champagne. She was sprawled on the floor, her head resting against his good knee. He sat on the sofa, the letter open in front of him. Monica said "Yes," and so he answered, "Good. Then I'll begin." He started to read aloud in his reading-aloud voice, a cross he liked to think, between John Gielgud and Anna Ford.

After the first paragraph, which Bognor had already taken in the letter moved on to some only mildly interesting generalizations about "life" as seen from Sir Roderick's side of the fence. "You will observe from the above" he wrote, "that there is virtually no one, even among my closest colleagues, so-called friends, and even family whom I do not despise, distrust, detest or at the very best, dislike."

"Cor," said Monica, "what an admission! Quite a turn of phrase for a disgusting old plutocrat."

There followed a paragraph each on those who were alleged to be his nearest and dearest. These were real ear-burners, though they did little more than confirm Bognor's own impressions. The extent of Farquhar's hatreds was perhaps surprising but the general assessment was much as he had supposed. After this bilious catalogue, the deceased briefly described his own illnesses. Bognor, ever squeamish, skipped this bit which was included, as far as he could see, simply to indicate that Sir Roderick had little time left, and knew it.

"And so you see, Mr. Bognor," he wrote, "I find myself faced with only a few weeks, maybe days before I shuffle this mortal coil. And when I look about me I see nothing but those I loathe. So what am I to make of imminent death and a handful of enemies? A little game perhaps . . . but with a happy ending, for despite everything, I should like to be remembered as having a sense of humour and a heart of gold."

"He had that all right," exclaimed Monica. "Gold through and through. All gold from his top to his toes."

"Hush," said Bognor. "This is where it's about to get interesting. Listen: 'I therefore concocted a plan. As you have seen there is scarcely one among those I have mentioned who does not have a reason to wish me dead. Amos would like the horses; Jean-Claude would like me out of the way for obscure political reasons I scarcely understand; Eleanor despite the ties of blood prefers my odious son-in-law whom I threaten by cutting her out of my will; little Crombie, of course, and poor Dolores . . . but all this you know. I repeat myself.

" 'My plan is this. There is to be a dinner party. A last farewell. No one knows quite how ill I am. Many of them believe there are a few years in me yet. The dinner will be lavish. Drinks will be consumed in quantity. As soon as coffee is served the lights will fail. Confusion reigns. There is a search for candles. Everyone, remember, is drunk. Suddenly there is a crash of breaking glass and when order is restored I'll be found seventeen stories away, facedown on the sidewalk. Not a very pleasant way to go but quick, or so I'm told. After that you should know the rest. I hope that by the time you come to read this you yourself will have been led a merry dance and my enemies will have had occasion to sweat a little. Only one, I presume, will have actually been charged with my murder and he may be released now that you are in possession of this "my confession." ' "

Bognor stopped.

"Are you," he asked his wife, "thinking what I'm thinking?"

"I can't imagine I'm thinking anything else," she said softly.

"In other words," he said, "it wasn't suicide at all."

"Doesn't he say anything about that bloody bath oil?" she asked.

"Hang on," he said, "there's more." He carried on reading. " 'If, as I suspect, no charge is brought and my death remains an unsolved mystery I shall have achieved my ambition. A question mark will hang over each person who attended that fatal dinner. Perhaps your unique capacity for getting things wrong will triumph. I expect that. Your spectacular misapprehensions over the Gentleman's Relish lead me to believe that you will blunder into making an arrest for a crime which was never committed. I hope you will agree that it was neatly set up. They all had motives. They all had opportunities. And because none of them are guilty all are equally guilty. Therefore you had better unarrest whoever it is that you have had the folly to charge. I wonder who it is, and I would like to think that wherever I go from here I shall be allowed at least the chance of finding out.

" 'I hope that I have caused as much anguish and distress in my leaving of life as I have in my living of it.

" 'With kind regards,

" 'Yours sincerely,

" 'Roderick Farquhar Bart.' "

"I'd no idea he was a baronet," said Bognor. "Plain 'Kt.' I think that's a con."

Monica said nothing for a while. Then she got up, fetched the Cliquot bottle and replenished their glasses. "That is *the* most extraordinary letter I have ever read," she said.

"Pretty odd," agreed Bognor. He watched the bubbles rising. "So that whole bath oil business was a complete red herring?"

"Not at all. It killed him. It was the bath oil that got him."

"No, but . . ." Bognor wanted to write things down. It was the only way he could marshal his thoughts. On the other hand his good leg had gone to sleep and his bad one was still stiff.

"You couldn't get a pencil and a notebook, could you?" he asked her quite nicely. "I can't move."

She did as she was asked. "I still think," she said, "that the bath oil was a plant."

"How do you mean?"

"Well, it's still just as peculiar as it was in the first place. It's his own personal, exclusive, nobody-else-for-the-use-of, boring bath oil. That's the first fact." She glanced at her husband. "Have you written that down?"

"Sort of."

"Well, you'd better, because it's important."

Bognor wrote, then frowned. "It's only *really* peculiar if you know that he was going to be killed with bath oil," he said plaintively. "It's quite normal if you don't know that. So if Farquhar didn't know that he was going to be killed with the stuff then there is nothing out of the way about giving it to people for Christmas."

"But," persisted Monica, "if he or A. N. Other knew, then it's peculiar again."

"Agreed," Bognor wrote furiously, "but it wasn't himself because we know that he was going to throw himself out of the window.

"He could have changed his mind," said Bognor. "He was obviously barking mad."

"Not especially," said Monica. "Just nasty."

"Hmmm." Bognor sucked the end of the pencil. "Let's leave him out of it for a moment. Who else in the world could have organized Balenciaga for Christmas?"

"Prideaux," said Monica, "obviously. Amos Littlejohn obviously controlled the supplies but he wouldn't be responsible for deciding on appropriate Christmas presents. I doubt it would be him."

"Fair enough. What about the others? We can rule Baker right out. And Crombie and the Bentleys. What about Eleanor or La Bandanna? He might have taken advice from them."

"Or your friend Maggie Fox." Bognor didn't care for the way Monica said her name. It made him feel a frisson of guilt. Quite unfairly. "They were still madly in love around Christmas," she continued, "or so she says. She seems to be rather keen on being madly in love."

"The whole point," Bognor spoke witheringly, "is that she *wasn't* madly in love with him. She refused to marry him. Remember?"

"Yes." Monica was grudging.

"Talking of her, she wants to talk to *me*. She turned up. She'd been missing."

"Oh, really." Monica stood up again and smoothed her dress. "I'm going to heat up those exotic thingies," she said. "You'd better phone Smith and tell him what's happened. He's going to be thrilled. First he's murdered, then he's a suicide, then he's murdered again. Next thing, he'll turn up alive and laughing and telling us all it's one big joke."

"Ha bloody ha," said Bognor. He poured the last of the champagne into his glass, and phoned Smith.

It was not a very happy conversation. The man from the Mounties was on the point of leaving his office for a game of racquetball with one of his colleagues. He had just completed his report of the affair for his bosses and regarded it as signed, sealed and all but delivered.

"Jeez, Si," he complained. "What are you doing to me? I mean, like, this is crazy. You're gonna have to come out with this letter and show it to our people. I mean, they are not going to believe this."

"I'm not sure I believe it myself," said Bognor. "I've always believed the dead should rest in peace but Farquhar seems determined not to."

"He sure is giving us a hard time from wherever he is," said Smith. "Also I have to tell you that the Baker broad is giving us trouble. She says she has a story to tell only you're the only guy she'll tell it to. She won't talk to me or Gary or anyone. Only you."

"That's going to be popular around here," said Bognor, thinking apprehensively of Monica.

"Can't help that, Si. From where I'm sitting you just have to get back on the next plane and come right back here."

"But that imbecile Baker's still gunning for me."

"Could be Baker. Could be those French bastards."

"Either way," said Bognor, "it's exceedingly dangerous."

"That's the name of the game, Si. Duty calls. You Brits know all about that. You're just gonna have to button down that lip and get on out. Leave your wife this time."

"Yes," he said, with feeling. "Listen I'll call you in the morning when I've spoken to the boss. Okay?"

"Sure, Si. Be seeing you."

And Bognor went off to the kitchen to eat warmed up gourmet beef bourguignonne and drink Rioja red with his long suffering wife.

CHAPTER 15

He had not expected to see Toronto again so soon. He sat in the back of the limo as it creamed down the airport expressway, and watched the dreaded CN Tower loom before him. It seemed years since he and Monica had been trapped in that terrifying little capsule so high above the city. Now from the cocoon of his well-heated Chevrolet Impala the tower looked only bizarre, a trademark of a space-age city, no threat to anyone, only a folly of self-esteem, or self promotion. Certainly not dangerous. Indeed Bognor viewed it with something approaching affection. He and it had been through a lot together. He was not going up again, but from ground level and at a respectful distance the two of them could be friends. He sighed. He did hope that this was going to be a less action-packed visit.

At the hotel there were two messages. One was from Smith, the other from Maggie Fox. His slight feeling of letdown was caused, he realized, because there was none from Louise Poitou. There was no reason why there should be. Rather the reverse. And before arriving it had not consciously occurred to him that he would see her or hear from her. Indeed it would be better, probably, if he did not. That way, he feared, lay trouble, but he knew too, that he invited trouble and, if the truth were told, rather enjoyed it. He was on the point of elevating it to a principle of life. Nevertheless he was not only surprised to feel let down, but rather shocked by the reason.

His room was not the same but similar. Identical in fact. Two floors lower and a few yards to the left, but the view of the harbour and the towers of Toronto was the same. So were the furniture, the wallpaper and the glossy magazine proclaiming the cosmopolitan delights of the city. He tipped the bellhop, sat down

on the bed and debated which call to make first. He opted for
Maggie. Smith could be postponed. Indefinitely for preference.
He dialled the number, and was surprised to hear a small Quebec-
oise voice answer.

"Louise?" he asked.

"Who's calling?"

"It's me. Bognor. Simon Bognor. Board of Trade."

"Oh." She sounded very guarded.

"Is Maggie with you? I had a message to call her."

"Of course. One moment."

Oh, well, thought Bognor. All for the best. He liked to be
friends though, and she sounded only just this side of hostile.

"Si, hi."

He was beginning to wish they didn't call him Si all the time.

"Hello. Maggie?"

"Yeah. Say, you and I have to talk. Are you in town?"

"Yes. I got your message. That's why I'm ringing."

"Oh. Okay. Listen, I'll be right over."

"Hang on. Hang on." Bognor was suddenly terrified. "Your
husband. That baboon who tried to do me in with a Chivas bottle. If you come here he'll be round with another mob of heavies."

"I understand you have protection, Si. Also I believe he's a little more in the picture now. I can't guarantee anything but . . .
well, look, we'll talk when I see you. Okay. I'll be with you in
thirty minutes. Maybe less."

Bognor hung up. He wondered if Baker knew he was back in
town. Baker obviously had eyes everywhere and he would be virtually certain to be having his wife followed. Or would he?
Maybe he had finally got the message and thrown in the sponge.
Bognor decided to err on the side of caution. He dialled Smith.

"Hello, Pete," he said, "may I have Gary back?"

"Oh." Smith seemed surprised. "Is that necessary? Are you
planning on walking into more trouble?"

"I have Mrs. Baker coming to see me. My experience is that
she brings trouble."

"You want a witness, eh, Si?" Smith chuckled. "Okay. I'll send
Gary along. Anything else?"

"I don't know. I have the letter. It depends on what Maggie Fox has to say."

"She surely wasn't saying anything to me, Si." Smith sounded envious. "That's some girl," he said.

"Let's hope she knows something," said Bognor. "I suppose you've released our friend the French bastard."

"That hurt. That hurt real bad."

"Never mind." Absurdly, Bognor felt guilty at depriving Smith of his victim, even though he had nothing to do with the murder. Or the suicide. Why should a man write a suicide note announcing his imminent death by defenestration, only to gas himself in the bath? Would it ever be solved? He doubted it.

"I don't trust the guy," said Smith.

"I don't trust any of these people. No more than I trusted Farquhar. But that doesn't mean to say you can arrest them all for murder."

"Pity."

"I agree." He did too.

Mrs. Baker, alias Maggie Fox, arrived only a few minutes later. He found it hard to think of her as any man's wife, let alone Baker's. In the same way that he himself had appeared married even when single, so she seemed incorrigibly unattached despite all evidence to the contrary. He said he would come down to the foyer when she called on the house telephone. Inviting her up to his room was the sort of gesture which her husband might misunderstand.

"Hallo," he said, lamely.

"Hi," she said. She had luminous lips today. They were smeared with shining pink lipstick which glowed in the dusk of the hotel lobby and she kept them permanently parted, the better, he decided, to display her teeth. Her white trousers were skintight. So was the angora sweater. Her toenails were painted and prominently displayed since the flimsy, high-heeled, sling-back sandals had no toe caps.

"Drink?" he asked. "We can find a quiet corner in the bar."

"Sure," she said.

Bognor guided her to the Anne Boleyn Room, where the hostess showed them to a secluded spot behind a bank of greenery. Maggie ordered a large milk, Bognor a scotch.

"I have a confession," she said, crossing and recrossing her legs. She was, he realized with a start of surprise, very nervous. He would have thought nervousness alien to her. She was far too self-possessed.

"A confession?"

"Yeah. I hope you won't think too badly of me." She passed the tip of her tongue along fluorescent lips. They looked far too moist to be dry.

Their drinks arrived. Maggie's milk was decorated with a large strawberry which she removed and ate before sucking at her straw. Bognor regarded her over the rim of his glass and waited. She looked back at him and smiled as she drank. Bognor sipped and went on waiting.

"I must seem just awful," she said eventually, licking her lips again. There was a thin moustache of white running above the fluorescent pink.

"You said you had a confession?" he offered, helpfully.

"Yeah."

"Well?"

"You remember I told you I had an affair with Sir Roderick?"

"I'd hardly forget."

She blushed. "That's not . . . well, that's not all."

Bognor frowned. He was being as helpful and sympathetic as he knew how. Obviously that wasn't helpful enough. He was out of his depth.

"I'm in love with Jean-Claude." She said it very quickly, then went back to her milk, avoiding his gaze.

"Present tense?" It seemed a reasonable enough question.

"Is that all you can say?" she flared.

He shrugged. "I'm sorry," he said, "I don't mean to appear insensitive. I just wondered how long you'd been . . . 'in love' . . . with Jean-Claude and whether you still were. It may affect what you have to say."

"I don't know," she said, confused now. "I really don't know. I have no idea."

"Suppose we start at the beginning," he said, "like last time. Only let's have the *whole* story."

She crossed her legs again and gave another embarrassed smile which accepted the memory of her previous confession.

"It was Farquhar first," she said. "What I told you at the zoo was true. He had a—I don't know, a quality I guess, that I found kinda irresistible."

"He was good in bed," said Bognor succinctly and harshly, "for a man of his age."

She sighed. "Okay," she acknowledged, "I suppose I asked for that. Any road, I had a relationship with him, and he asked me to marry him. I turned him down."

"Whereupon Farquhar sent your letters to your husband?"

"Uh, no. That was Jean-Claude."

"Why?"

"One, he was jealous. Two, he wanted to deflect my husband's suspicions."

"In which he succeeded?"

"Sure. No one knew about me and Jean-Claude. Not even Louise."

"Does she know now?"

"Yeah."

"And Baker—your husband?"

She concentrated on her milk. "I guess so," she said.

"Okay," said Bognor. "You were having an affair with Jean-Claude at the same time as you were having an affair with Farquhar. Meanwhile you were still married to Baker. Anyone else?"

"You make me sound terrible."

"*I* don't make you sound anything, Maggie. Anybody else?"

"Nobody else that matters."

Bognor signalled the waitress for another round of drinks. Maggie said she'd switch from milk and join him in a scotch.

"Go on," he said.

"He was killed with that goddam bath oil, right?"

"Right."

"That was Jean-Claude's idea."

"What? Killing him with it—or sending it out as Christmas presents?"

She leaned across the table. Talk of killing seemed to upset her. She lowered her voice to a whisper. "He suggested the Christmas presents. He said Farquhar was mean as hell and it would appeal to the Scrooge in him. It did."

"But did he kill him? And was it premeditated? I mean, did he know when he persuaded Farquhar to send them out at Christmas?"

She shook her head but in bewilderment rather than denial.

"I really don't know which came first," she said, "but I know he killed him."

"But why? Nothing to do with the Quebecois and Seven. Something to do with you."

"Yes. Yes." She drank gratefully from the scotch. "Roddie put cash into an account in our joint name. It wouldn't show in a will. Jean-Claude wanted to get his hands on it. If I had gone off with him I'd have been cut out by everyone: no cash from my husband, no cash from Roddie. And, by the way, no job for Jean-Claude."

"So Jean-Claude killed him and you kept the money in the joint account?"

"I kept the money from the joint account, but I didn't know that Jean-Claude had killed him. Not until . . . the other day." She blushed and stared at her scotch.

"What happened the other day?"

She took a deep breath. "I wanted to get shot of Jean-Claude. Like I told you, I'm not a one-guy gal, and I guess the time had come. Oh, God!" She took another drink. "I must seem so awful. I was fond of the guy, but . . . I don't want to settle down with him nor with anyone."

"You're not in love with him," Bognor groaned. "So you told him it was"—he searched his mind for the correct phrase and found it hidden among lines from bad movies—"all over between you."

"Yeah. And then he went berserk. He told me he'd killed for me and killed to get me and, I don't know, he was just insane. Would you believe he pulled a gun on me and he took me to that cottage he borrows on Ward's Island and he kept me there, tied up like an animal. He wouldn't let me go. I told him it was all over but he wouldn't listen."

"Oh." Bognor's mind raced. "You're sure he told you he killed Farquhar, you're not making it up this time?"

"I'm sure. He said he put some crystals in the bath oil when they were on the train. He threw the packet out of the window into some river. He was jealous and he wanted me to have the money. He knew that if I went off with him, Roddie would cancel the account."

Bognor slumped back in his chair. "Nothing to do with the PQ, the Group of Seven, Quebec, all that?"

"Nope. I don't think Jean-Claude cared about all that. But he felt humiliated by Roddie and he thought he could get even through me. Then he realized he couldn't have me without Roddie firing him and taking the money and . . ." She passed a palm over her forehead. "Don't ask me *why*. Why should anyone do such a thing under any circumstances? Take the life of another human. It's too terrible."

"Did you say you'd tell?"

"On him? Sure. That's why he kept me locked up. I thought he would maybe kill me too."

"And"—Bognor was experiencing palpitations—"you told him who you'd tell? I.e., me?"

"Sure." Maggie nodded enthusiastically. "I don't trust those Mounties."

Bognor nodded wanly. "Thanks very much," he said. "First your husband. Now your lover."

She looked surprised. How dumb is this blonde, he wondered, as she buried her face in her glass and looked up at him with suffering, misunderstood eyes.

"Gee," she said, "you don't think Jean-Claude would try to do anything to you?"

"Why not? I have a hunch he tried to murder us in the lift at the CN Tower."

She frowned. "You mean the elevator. He was just warning you off, trying to frighten you. He didn't mean any harm."

All around them the early evening ritual of the happy hour was

taking place. Men in elegant business suits were imbibing un-
winding sundowners before returning to the challenge of wife and
home. The atmosphere was ultracivilized, far far away from sudden death unless by coronary or cirrhosis.

"You're telling me that he murdered Farquhar, and made you a
prisoner. I should have thought he'd be bound to have a go at me
now he's been released."

"But surely now he'll have to be arrested again?" Maggie's eyes
were wider still. "He can't do anything to you. You *can* do something to him."

Bognor frowned. She was right. Or would have been if dealing
with a conventional relationship between policeman and suspect.
But somehow his life never panned out like that. He sighed and
looked at his watch. "Where the hell's Gary?" he said angrily.
"We'll need him. We have to find Jean-Claude and I am certainly not attempting that on my own."

He left the girl and went out into the lobby, where he saw
Gary standing at the desk in conversation with one of the assistant managers.

"Tried calling your room," said Gary, apologetically. "No reply.
So I was just going to have you paged."

"We're in the Anne Boleyn Room." Bognor spoke crisply, with
an air of urgency. "But before we go back I think we'd better call
Smith. Something's come up."

Together they crammed into one of the telephone booths, so
tiny that it had evidently been designed exclusively for visiting
Japanese. It was far too small for occidentals built on the scale of
Gary and Bognor.

"What's happened?" asked Gary. "Did the broad come
through?"

"Just listen," snapped Bognor, glad that he had Gary between
him and the unknown menace from the outside world, only wishing that he weren't quite so close. He could feel his heartbeat.

Smith's reaction, when Bognor managed to communicate the
full import of Maggie's revelation, was much as one might expect.
After the initial silence there was a sound of low moaning followed by a choke and then the words, "Jesus wept!"

"I'm sorry, Pete," said Bognor.

"Is that all you can say? We nailed the bastard. We had him in here. Despite everything I pulled the bastard in. Then you tell me he didn't do it on account of there wasn't no murder after all so I let the bastard free and now you turn round and say he did do it. And then you say you're sorry. What in hell am I gonna tell Ottawa?"

"Don't tell them anything yet. Let's rearrest him first."

"That's not so damned easy," said the Mountie. "The guy will have split. Where do you imagine he will be, sitting on his ass back home eating frogs' legs? He'll be in Paris, France, or some such place."

"I doubt it," said Bognor. "I should imagine he'll be feeling supremely lucky and untouchable by now. Not often a guilty man is arrested and then released without even being charged."

"Don't remind me, Si," said Smith. "I don't wanna know."

"Well, I suggest you come and pick us up and we'll all go looking for him."

"Okay." Smith sounded disapproving and world weary. Bognor sympathised, though try as he might, he could not feel as much guilt as he was obviously supposed to.

"We'd better send Mrs. Baker home," he said to Gary as they moved back to the Anne Boleyn Room. "This could be unpleasant. Especially for her, though underneath all that ingenue eye fluttering and breast heaving I sense that she is, as you would say, 'one tough cookie.'"

Gary grinned.

Smith arrived ten minutes later in an unmarked white Chevrolet which came into the hotel forecourt with a squeal of rubber and crash-stopped inches short of two doormen dressed, for no immediately apparent reason, as Yeomen of the Guard. Maggie Fox had left five minutes earlier, tearful and confused. Bognor could not really make out whether she was extremely sinister or amazingly silly, though it crossed his mind that the two were not mutually exclusive.

"Hi," he said to Smith who was sitting in the front passenger seat wearing his Tip Top Tailor suit and a face like frost.

"In the back, you two," said Smith. "We gotta move!" Gary was already in the back seat. Bognor fell in beside him and the car leapt away before he could even shut the door. One of the Yeomen of the Guard did it for him as they spun past.

"Junction of Bloor and Spadina," said Smith, ultralaconically.

The driver merely nodded.

Bognor, feeling that he had drifted into a dangerous alien world, noticed that he was the only man not chewing gum. Also the only one without the bulge under his jacket which meant firearms. Lame and defenceless, he picked a duty-free cheroot from the pack in his pocket, stuffed it in his mouth and tried to feel virile. No one spoke. From time to time the car's shortwave radio set crackled, but it said nothing that was intelligible to him. He sat back, chewed the cigar and stared out into the evening cold.

"That's it," said Smith suddenly, nodding towards an anonymous grey mass of concrete. The car mounted the pavement and crunched to another jolting halt. As it did the two Mounties jumped out and ran to the glass doors, where they halted, looking foolish, and began a conversation with the automatic answering device set in the wall. As Bognor wandered up to join them an elderly caretaker in a shabby peaked cap walked slowly across the vestibule and made elaborately hard work of opening the doors. When he had done so Smith thrust an ID card under his nose as menacingly as if it had been a Smith and Wesson, and barged past. Bognor, struggling in the policemen's wake, smiled ingratiatingly.

"Sorry," he said, "bit of a flap on. We're looking for Mr. Prideaux."

"Not in," said the doorman in a tortured Central European accent. Latvian, Bognor speculated with the disengaged portion of his brain.

"Not in?" said Bognor. The Mounties had sprung into the elevator in a few electric bounds. The panel above its entrance indicated that they were already passing the eighth floor. "Why not?"

"He went out," said the Latvian.

"Out? Where to? How long ago? Who with?"

The old man backed away from him, mouth sagging in incomprehension.

Bognor spoke very slowly and carefully.

"How long ago did he leave?"

The old man consulted his watch and gave the question some thought. "Twenty minutes," he said. "Maybe half an hour."

"And was he on his own?"

The caretaker shook his head excitedly. "He was with three men. They are not friends of Mr. Prideaux. He not like very much. They hurt him I think."

"What did they look like, these men?"

"Very big." He held his hands wide to indicate size. "Very big," he repeated. "They are strong, strong like so." He gripped a puny bicep in further demonstration. "Two of them, they hold on to Mr. Prideaux very tight. They not want to lose him. He not want to go."

"These men," Bognor articulated. "They look . . ." He faltered, trying to remember the thugs who had abducted him from Toronto Metro Zoo, and then wondering how on earth he was to describe them in pidgin. "They look very tough. Very ugly. Like wrestlers maybe."

The man nodded with enthusiasm. "Right, right," he said. "Not good men."

Bognor glanced up at the numbered lights. They showed that the lift had come to rest on the twenty-first floor. He might as well wait, he decided. They would discover that their bird had flown soon enough and there was not the remotest point in flogging all the way to the twenty-first floor just to tell them what they knew already. They would have to come back down in any case. Bognor thanked his Latvian friend and gave him five dollars. He smiled a thank-you, displaying a great many gold teeth, and shuffled away, shaking his head and muttering. Seconds later Bognor observed the descent of the elevator, and was pleased to see his two colleagues emerge with rueful expressions.

"Not there," said Smith. "Didn't answer so we broke the door down. Seemed to have been some sort of fight. Lamps broken. Blood on the carpet."

"He left about half an hour ago," Bognor told them, smugly, "and I'm afraid my guess is that he's been abducted by Baker's boys. Like I was."

"Like you were, Si?" Smith was so surprised by this revelation that he stopped chewing for an instant. "By *Baker*? Do you mean the Baker I mean, Si?"

"The Honourable John."

"Oh, Jeez, Si." Smith sat down on a plush sofa and wiped his brow. "That's a terrible thing to say."

"That's why I didn't say it before."

"You were right not to. Why in hell go and say it now?"

"Because," Bognor weighed his words to make them count. "Because my bet is that Baker has abducted Prideaux and if he has then I think Prideaux is in serious danger."

"Aw, c'mon Si, you're not serious."

"Never more so. Baker is paranoid. *And* impotent. If he thinks Prideaux has been having an affair with his wife he'll have his guts for garters."

Smith scratched his head.

"You mean this, Si?"

"Yes. Baker bloody near broke my skull. He threw a bottle of Chivas at me."

"Go on."

"I think he's got Prideaux and I think we have to go and find out."

"We can't just go barging in there, Si, that guy may be the next Prime Minister of Canada."

"I hope not."

"Yeah, but . . . Si, I got a family. I mean, I don't think I can take the sort of risk you're asking me to."

Bognor saw his point of view. It was an embarrassing situation. "Listen," he said. "It would give me a lot of pleasure to see Baker again with the boot on the other foot. I'll do all the necessary talking. You two just back me up. Make it clear you're RCMP, and armed."

"I don't like it, Si."

"Do you want to find Prideaux?"

"Guess so, Si, but . . ."

"Okay," said Simon, "let's go." At last he was feeling quite genuinely virile. Those latent powers of leadership, usually dormant, were suddenly showing signs of life and he was delighted to see that the two men, despite obvious misgivings, were going to acquiesce in his plans. They returned to the Chevy and clambered in.

"You know John Baker's place, mac?" enquired Smith.

The driver nodded. "Sure. Rosedale."

"Okay. Take us there. Fast."

He was a highly skilled driver and despite heavy traffic and more ice on the roads than salt and grit could quite remove he did the trip in only a few minutes. Once as they paused briefly for a red light, a city policeman on his old Harley-Davidson and sidecar drew up to ask what in hell they thought they were doing, careening down the wrong side of Bloor on the wrong side of sixty. Smith waved his card and the motorcyclist shrugged with ill-tempered resignation as he vanished into their slipstream.

There were several parked cars in the driveway of Baker's mansion: Cadillacs, Lincolns and a couple of Rolls-Royces.

"Party time," said Bognor laconically.

"You sure you want to go through with this, Si?" asked Smith, falteringly. "Looks like we picked a bad time."

"Don't be silly," snapped Bognor. "It's the best possible time. He'll hardly risk a scene with all these people in the house."

They waited, shivering by the front door for a full minute, then it was opened by a servant in black jacket and tie.

"Mr. Baker?" asked Bognor, exaggerating the Englishness of his accent.

"Mr. Baker is tied up right now."

"Well, I'd be obliged if you'd untie him. Sharpish."

"I . . ." The flunkey seemed on the point of shutting the door but something about Bognor's manner, or more likely the armed menace of the two Mounties flanking him, made him change his mind. "I'll see," he said. "Who shall I say?"

"Bognor. Board of Trade, London, England. And my colleagues here are from the Royal Canadian Mounted Police."

The man hesitated. "You'd better come in, gentlemen," he said. "If you care to wait in the hall I'll see if Mr. Baker is available."

From somewhere down a corridor they could hear party sounds, conversation hum, laughter.

"I'm not happy about this," said Smith, shifting unhappily from one foot to the other. "This could finish me."

"Relax," said Bognor. "It's far more likely to finish him."

"Jesus, Si," Smith hissed, "you're a Brit, maybe you don't understand. This guy is like, important."

"Never heard of him until a few weeks ago," said Bognor, "but hush, here comes his master's voice."

Indeed the flunkey was returning.

"Mr. Baker will see you now," he said flatly. "This way." And he led them down a passage and into the long study with the photographs and Maple Leaf flag that Bognor remembered so well from his previous encounter. Baker was sitting behind his desk as before. He did not stand to receive them, nor did he give the slightest sign of recognition. However, Bognor was sure he was not mistaken. He knew. And Baker knew he knew. But how to prove it?

"What can I do for you, gentlemen?" he asked. "I hope it's important. I'm entertaining some old friends of mine. I can give you five minutes."

"We're looking for Prideaux." Bognor saw no point in messing around. He felt Smith flinch. Baker, on the other hand, did not blink.

"I don't understand," he said, coolly. "There must be some mistake."

"Prideaux," repeated Bognor. "Jean-Claude Prideaux, onetime private secretary to Sir Roderick Farquhar of the Mammon Corporation and lover of your wife, Margaret."

Bognor had to admire the man's self-possession. He scarcely blinked. But he knew. Bognor knew he knew.

Instead of responding directly Baker turned to Smith, who was sweating visibly.

"Who is this guy?" he asked. "I let you guys in because you're from the RCMP. I have time and respect for the RCMP but I don't expect to be insulted in their presence by some goddamn English faggot."

"That's what you said last time we met." Bognor was stung. "I very much hope nothing has happened to Mr. Prideaux because if it has you're in trouble, no matter who your friends are."

Baker stood and addressed his next remark to Smith.

"Lookit," he said, "I'm a busy man. I'm sure you two Mounties are busy men as well. So why don't you remove this phoney and let's all get back to our busy lives, eh?"

"If you think you'll get away with this, Baker," said Bognor, wagging a finger at the corrupt tycoon, "you've got another think coming. You're an impotent psychopath. Did you throw a bottle of Chivas at Prideaux too? Eh? Eh?"

Baker flicked at his jacket as if to remove alien fluff.

"Good night, gentlemen," he said. "I've heard enough. I'll make no formal complaint this time since you're obviously as embarrassed by this lunacy as I am."

With which he spun on his heel and exited, leaving the servant to usher them out, much discomfitted.

"You sure blew that one, Si," said Smith, when they were out in the winter again.

"He's a good liar, I'll grant you that," said Bognor. "But *what* a liar. God!"

"So now what do we do?" asked Gary. "Feller Prideaux is still missing and we know he was taken out by three guys against his inclinations. We gotta find him, eh, Chief?"

"Sure," concurred Smith. But he said no more. The three men got into the car where they remained, brooding.

"Hey!" Bognor felt a sudden tingling down his back. "Where did you say they found me after those gorillas roughed me up?"

"On the Don Valley," said Smith, "under one of the bridges. Do you remember, Gary? The Danforth, or was it higher? St. Clair maybe?"

"Don't remember," said Gary, "but it was on the Parkway. The suicide place."

"'Sright," said Smith.

"Let's go there," said Bognor. "Now."

Smith exhaled. He seemed to sag in the middle as if punctured. "Why not?" he said. "We've been halfway round the city already. Then we'll call back at Prideaux's apartment. The bastard's tucked up in bed by now, I guess."

Gary laughed dutifully.

"Don Valley Parkway first," said Bognor. He had a nasty feeling in the pit of his stomach. They were such morons. The odds were that they would use the same dumping ground a second time. He was certain Prideaux was in their hands and he was equally certain that Prideaux was not going to be let off with a warning. Bognor's sin had been denied and unproven. Not Prideaux's. He had an idea that Baker's men had done the state's duty before the state could do it for itself.

The car sped along Rayview before looping round onto the parkway which ran north-south along the valley. Traffic was heavy. Endless automobiles speeding along with no thought for the slippery frostbitten surface.

"Slower," said Bognor, "please."

The driver pulled into the inside lane and reduced speed. Bognor stared hard out of the window. They passed under one high viaduct.

"Nothing there," said Smith. He too was gazing out, looking for a corpse. He did not expect to find one. Bognor did.

They passed under another bridge, very slowly this time, not more than twenty miles an hour. Behind them a car flashed its lights and sounded its horn. They were beginning to cause a jam.

"Nope," said Smith.

They drove on. There was no bridge for a mile or more. The tension in the car began to relax. Bognor felt in his pocket for a cigar. Smith coughed. A heavy articulated truck with Quebec number plates screamed past, obliterating the windscreen with a spray of slush. The driver flicked the windscreen wipers into top gear and swore quietly.

"There!" shouted Bognor, pointing. "The lights. Pull over."

"Been a shunt," said Smith. The flashing lights were from a police car. Or an ambulance. In fact, both, as they realized when they got close.

"Just a shunt," said Smith again, but there was a tightness in his voice which warned Bognor that he did not believe it.

They pulled up just short of the flashing lights. The door of the ambulance was open. On the ground just behind it there was a stretcher. On the stretcher was a shape. The shape was covered in blankets or rugs. Even as they walked towards the scene one of the ambulance men pulled a blanket towards the head of the

stretcher and let it fall so that it—him—whatever it was, lay totally obscured beneath.

Smith showed his ID card to the city policeman in charge, a
young lieutenant with sandy hair and a Scots accent.

"Suicide," said the lieutenant. "Chucked himself off the
bridge." He glanced up at the parapet several hundred feet above.
"He wouldn't have known much about it."

"Any identification?"

"Name of Prideaux. Jean-Claude Prideaux."

There was a silence. The only sound was the constant swoosh
of the traffic as it hurried past, the living mocking the dead.

"Did he fall, Officer?" asked Bognor. "Or was he pushed?"

The policeman glanced at him suspiciously.

"I'd assume suicide, sir," he said. "It's a favourite spot. And
with respect it would be impossible to tell one way or another.
He's a hell of a mess. I'd guess a dozen or so automobiles . . .
Well, I don't need to spell it out for you."

"No." Bognor coughed. He went back to the car and sat in the
back, his face between his knees. There but for the grace of the
God in whom I don't believe . . . he kept thinking. A moment or
so later Gary and Pete Smith returned. The car started up, and
slid away into the traffic. Bognor remembered that earlier noctur-
nal excursion on the city's highways in the little green Pinto after
the dreadful rendition of *The Mousetrap*. He swallowed hard.
Prideaux had not been likeable, but even so . . .

In the front Pete Smith turned to face Bognor.

"Guess I owe you an apology, Si," he said, and when Bognor
failed to answer, he added, very softly, "Poor French bastard,
eh?"

EPILOGUE

There was no prosecution. There was no proof. Bognor knew and Baker knew Bognor knew, but Baker was beyond reach. He was too strong and the evidence was too weak. Bognor filed a report. A copy for Parkinson. A copy for the RCMP. It was the least he could do. It would only gather dust but at least it was in the archives. Someone might exhume it one day. It might just put the skids under Baker's headier political aspirations.

He himself broke the news to Maggie Fox. She appeared quite distressed but by now Bognor was past caring about her distress, real or imaginary. Emotion, he realized, was not her forte. Louise was at the flat. It was, after all, her flat. Afterwards she showed him out. If anything she was more shattered than Maggie, though she made no display of her shock and sadness. She looked wan and vulnerable and disturbingly attractive. So much so that standing by her front door Bognor was moved to say,

"That dinner. I suppose you wouldn't revive your acceptance?"

She managed a weak smile. She had had no idea about Jean-Claude, had not suspected about him and Maggie, let alone the murder. She was an innocent.

"I don't think so," she said. "It's kind of you, but I think you should go home to your wife, don't you?"

But she kissed him all the same, to show no hard feelings. Bognor found it upsetting, but he did as he was told.

Pete and Gary came to the airport to see him off. He was touched by this too.

"Sorry," he said. "Wasn't much use really, was I?"

Smith pumped his hand up and down with enthusiasm. "Lookit, Si," he said. "We had a ball. Eh?"

Gary said, "Have a good flight, sir."

After the plane took off it circled over the city. Bognor looked down at the sparkling lights, tried to work out which road was which, located Yonge and then realized he was mistaken. Only the dark line of the lake gave him a certain reference, and there, poised as always for blast-off, was the winking light of the CN Tower. Bognor gazed back at it wistfully, remembering Monica and himself hurtling down its side in that deadly yellow capsule. He smiled at the light and winked back.

"O Canada!" he said.

Tim Heald has written five previous novels featuring Simon Bognor: *Let Sleeping Dogs Die, Deadline, Unbecoming Habits, Blue Blood Will Out* and *Just Desserts*. He is also the author of the recently published novel *Caroline R* and, with Mayo Mohs, a biography of Prince Charles called *HRH: The Man Who Will Be King*. As a journalist, he has written numerous profiles of such subjects as the British royal family, Pierre and Margaret Trudeau, and Richard Burton. He lives in Surrey, England, with his wife and four children. *Murder at Moose Jaw* is his first novel for the Crime Club.